FOUR TUBES, FOUR TORPEDOES, FOUR SHIPS . . .

S.S. *Harpel* was ripped apart . . . A ship in the fifth column went up in a single fantastic ball of fire . . . a torpedo claimed a tanker . . . further explosions erupted from the convoy . . .

Men covered in oil were burning in the sea.

Hands, faces, bare chests, all were burning, frizzling, frying.

A few survivors were hauled in over the side.

The sight of these men, half-naked, burned, dying, wounded, struck deeply into the mind of Lieutenant-Commander Raymond, R.N. He watched as they were taken below. He wondered how many of them, if any, would survive.

And still the slaughter went on . . .

SHARK PACK
#3

BRUNO KRAUSS

ZEBRA BOOKS
KENSINGTON PUBLISHING CORP.

ZEBRA BOOKS

are published by

KENSINGTON PUBLISHING CORP.
475 Park Avenue South
New York, N.Y. 10016

Printed in the United States of America

CHAPTER ONE

Oberleutnant zur See Baldur Wolz stared hungrily across the moon-hazed sea at the convoy, like – and here he felt a quick sharp pleasure at the cruel image – like a savage beast of the jungle at the water hole, glaring down upon its prey. U-55 stalked the convoy, her lean grey steel flanks quivering with the power of her diesels and the running wash of the sea. She moved in for the first kill.

Only a slight swell disturbed the surface of the Atlantic and under an intermittently overcast sky, visibility was good up to four or five miles.

A flowering rose of fire broke and bloomed upward from the starboard side of the convoy. Moments later, the concussion reached Wolz and the men on the bridge of U-55. The boat heaved only momentarily, the conning tower rolling, and then surged on, a long grey steel shark carrying death and destruction to the enemies of the Third Reich.

'Someone's already at work,' commented Wolz. The thin black cheroot thrust aggressively up from the corner of his wide mouth, the thin lips firmed down, clamped. The cigar was unlit. He stared again past the flanks of the convoy under the moon. 'Now it's our turn.'

The lookouts kept their unceasing watch to all points of the compass. All knew what their skipper would say to them if they could not resist the temptation to turn and stare in fascination at the glowing, blood-red sight of a British tanker burning.

The damned English destroyers raced about the flanks of the compact lines of merchantmen like sheepdogs around their flock and every U-boat man on bridge watch must keep his eyes skinned down to the very limits of vision to sight them first. Baldur Wolz shared the confidence of his fellow U-boat skippers that he could take the long low shape of his boat in close without being seen. U-55 lay low in the water, trimmed down, every now and then a wave breaking along the casing of her foredeck and creaming in a welter of suds about the 8.8 centimetre gun and the base of the conning tower. He knew he would see the English destroyers first – provided the lookouts kept alert. If the U-boat men did not spot the English first, he'd likely be taking a swim, rammed and rolled over and sunk.

No further explosions followed that first horrific destruction of the tanker.

The moon slid behind a flying wedge of overcast and darkness clamped sea and sky. U-55 plunged on. Wolz braced on the bridge; his mind grappled with the calculations that would place him in the perfect position for a shot.

Not overly tall, Baldur Wolz, but big and broad-shouldered, with a square, sharp-featured German face, and an immaculately-combed head of blond hair. His pale grey-blue eyes strove to pierce the darkness, and he chewed on that evil cigar, and drove his boat along.

Menace breathed in the air and sea. Menace from the guns and depthcharges and sharp steel prows of the English destroyers, menace from the torpedoes in the forrard tubes, ready to run, loosed from the U-boats to smash through thin steel plating, opening in explosion and violence the ships to the sea.

Wolz conned U-55 in closer. A shredding drift of cloud allowed the moon to shaft through, pallidly illuminating the smoothly swelling surface of the sea and the ships struggling upon that naked surface.

'Steer one-two-five.'

'Steer one-two-five,' came the answering voice from the quartermaster in the kiosk below Wolz.

He took up his night glasses and studied the forma-

6

tion of the English ships as he had studied them all during this run up. Four U-boats had been called together by BdU and already one had struck. Admiral Donitz was able, in this high summer of 1940, to put into practice his firmly-held beliefs in the concentrated attack. Now Wolz was being given his chance to be a part of a wolf pack, and to strike with his fellow U-boat commanders.

Down in the kiosk, with his eye glued to the attack periscope eyepiece, Leutnant Ehrenberger read off the ranges and angles. During an attack on the surface, the skipper commanded from the bridge. The Number One handled the periscope. Now Wolz leaned forward, his jaw thrust out, sizing up the ships, selecting the fattest target available to him.

A tanker!

Yes, they were the fat ones, the ones that exploded with such a supernal blaze of brilliance across the night sky.

The English ships were ranged in six columns of five ships apiece – thirty merchantmen and tankers ploughing their way from Newfoundland to Liverpool, carrying all those things that England needed so desperately now that the war was to continue after it had, to all intents and purposes, been won by the armed forces of Germany.

The suspense of this attack, stealing up in the night, had to be combated. The tension of waiting until the right moment to loose the deadly eels; the knowledge that at any moment an English destroyer might loom up from the darkness and cut them in two; the knowledge that any one of a hundred tiny things in the complicated structure of the U-boat might choose that moment to malfunction – all these nerve-sapping thoughts must be pushed away. The attack alone mattered. That must be pushed home to the hilt.

Wolz spoke briskly to Ehrenberger.

'Can you see that tanker clearly, Kern?'

Kern was not Herr Leutnant Ehrenberger's real name; but it was what everybody called him.

'Yes, a nice fat juicy one.'

'Mind you hit him.'

7

'I hope he makes a bigger bang than the other.'

'How many degrees to go?'

Ehrenberger's voice came up after a brief pause.

'Fifteen.'

'Helmsman, steer one-one-oh.'

'Steer one-one-oh.'

'Torpedo tubes ready. Stand by, Number One.'

Every sound that rumbled and echoed through the boat and reached him up the hatch and through the soles of his shoes told Wolz what was going on. Bowcaps opened. The eels were ready.

He found bitter memories of the Norwegian campaign crowding in. There torpedoes had malfunctioned so regularly that they had become more than a joke. Gunther Prien of U-47 had given up in disgust and refused to hazard his boat shooting at a convoy of British troop transports with, as he had put it, a dummy rifle. The risks had not been worth it.

Now, with contact pistols fitted to the torpedoes in place of the magnetic type, the eels ought to work. U-55 had sailed on patrol and, vectored on to this convoy by BdU, was facing her first action under the command of her new skipper, Baldur Wolz.

Befehlshaber der Unterseeboote, BdU, hoped for much from the attacks carried out in concentrated operations. Wolz fully believed in them himself. As he took a lowering methodical look all around the compass, he wondered where the other two boats could be. One had struck. Now U-55 was going in. To take the fullest advantage of Rudel Taktik the boats should attack as closely together as possible.

'Coming on, Herr Oberleutnant –'

'Make sure of him, Kern.'

There appeared to have been no reaction from the convoy to the loss of the tanker. But appearances were deceptive.

Wolz gripped the coaming of the bridge in hands that bit like talons. Only a few more moments and they could shoot their four torpedoes. After that they could take all

8

the evasive action that might be necessary. Abaft the tanker and in the next column sailed a three-island freighter, and abreast of her another tall-stacked merchantman. The fourth eel was already marked in Wolz's mind for the ship laying a little way abaft them, at the tail of the convoy.

'Tubes Three, Four and Two ready!'

Come on, Kern, come on! Wolz quelled the thoughts. The time would be given by the attack table. Wolz stared viciously at the black hulks of the ships riding purposefully through the water. They were three quarters of a mile off, and at that range, the U-boat would be practically invisible from the English look-outs. He could judge the ranges and the angles himself, if it came to it . . . His fists gripped and he watched as the bows swung and the moon patched with cloud and the darkness swooped.

'Lost him!' called Ehrenberger. Exasperation quivered in the First Lieutenant's voice.

'Hold it, hold it,' said Wolz. 'I'll take it.'

In his mind's eye he could see the tanker and the other ships, could see the thin ghostly band of white foaming past his bows. Now!

'Loose!' he called, firmly, harsh with purpose.

With that thrilling thump of compressed air, the torpedo shot from the forrard tube. Wolz waiting, contained within himself, counting, said: 'Loose!'

Tube Number Three emptied of seventy thousand marks worth of destruction.

'Loose!'

Tube Number Four belched with compressed air.

Then, finally, triumphantly: 'Loose!'

Number Two shot clear of the bows of U-55.

'Steer one-eight-oh. Half ahead on both engines.'

U-55 swung about, heading out from the convoy but keeping in touch, moving off from the starboard bow.

Everyone waited.

'Four torpedoes running,' reported the hydrophone operator.

Wolz could feel his blood burning in him. His head

ached as though compressed. He stared towards the convoy, willing the eels to run true, the contact pistols to work. So much effort and agony had been expended, and good men dead; too much – far too much for it all to end in anticlimax.

The first explosion came just as the hand of the stop-watch clicked to the second of death.

The tanker ripped apart in the night.

An immense gusher of fire shot up. They must have caught her in a tender spot. Fire spread and rose, a gigantic ball, roaring and pulsating in the night. The whole convoy showed like small black beetles luridly illuminated down one side. The noise continued in bellowings and crackings, a wind-rushing gale of fire. The sea stained as though blood had spilled lavishly upon it.

In due order the next two explosions followed. This time the concussions were those of torpedoes. Wolz saw the tall glimmering-white columns rise. He saw the ships lurch. Three torpedoes and three hits and three strikes.

He felt the elation bubbling.

But the fourth?

The stopwatch clicked on and past and nothing reached the straining ears and eyes of the men in U-55.

With all the racket of underwater breaking and of water rushing in, there was little chance the hydrophone operator could pick up the soft, thumpy, dead sound of a torpedo hitting a ship's hull and failing to explode.

'Three out of four,' said Wolz. Despite his own high standards, he could not feel too displeased.

Down in the boat the men were thumping each other on the back and yelling. Wolz let them carry on their antics for a space. Morale was important and must be carefully nurtured.

Time enough to bear down on them if they appeared likely to let him down. Baldur Wolz was no skipper who would wait until the event before clamping down.

The convoy reacted. Flares erupted. The ships continued in their lines; but the lines broke and straggled as successive ships steered to avoid the holocaust in the water.

A destroyer appeared around the starboard flank of the convoy and went haring down, a bright bone of white water in her teeth.

Depth charges crumped.

Wolz smiled.

They were for morale, English morale. Designed to put a lurking U-boat down, to drive her off, they could do no damage to U-55, safely on the surface and over a mile away. The destroyer continued on, running swiftly over the calm sea, and her upperworks showed black and gaunt against the blazing bonfire of destruction within the convoy.

The destroyer was an old V and W class, tired and feeble, and should have been pensioned off. But Wolz was well aware that if she caught U-55 she could still sting, could still destroy them.

He bent to the voice-pipe.

'I wish to put in another attack on this convoy, Herr Leutnant Neitzel.' Wolz put drive and snap into his voice. 'Faster time than ever before!'

'Very good!'

Neitzel, the Third Officer, needed encouragement most of the time; but every now and then he needed a quick boot up the backside. Wolz decided this was one of those times.

'If you let the convoy get away through slowness, Herr Leutnant, I shall not be pleased.'

In the forward compartment, Neitzel and the torpedo crew would be sweating their guts out, ripping out the reloads, readying them for operation, juggling them into the tubes. That was hard, dirty, dangerous work. The only thing the torpedo men had going for them was the calmness of the sea.

Now was no time to submerge, with a convoy struggling to continue on course for England. If he dived now he'd lose them. After the very first tanker explosion, and then his own three attacks, there had been no further

11

onslaught. There were two other U-boats hungrily sniffing around the convoy. Chewing on his foul black cigar, Wolz wondered what was holding them up. No. Diving was out of the question. Neitzel would reload, and reload damn quick, on the surface.

Three thousand metres off on the port beam, the convoy moved through the night. Wolz paced their seven knots with ease, husbanding his diesels and his fuel.

Not for the first time, he reflected with great complacency on the luck that had brought Leutnant z. S. Loeffler to serve with him in U-55. It had been Loeffler who, with his genius with engines and machinery, had brought U-55 safely back from her grave in Norway. Abandoned by her original crew, and by Donitz's personal order salvaged by a hastily flown-in party from U-45, she had been refitted and brought back to operational condition. That had taken time. Wolz, as the second in command to Kapitanleutnant Adolf Forstner of U-45, had deliberately left the boil of a man back in Oslo and had gone flying off to Narvik without him. Rewards had flowed from that decisive action – and also ungentle and horrific deeds Wolz thought about only when he had to – and the chief of these rewards: command of a U-boat.

At last, Baldur Wolz commanded his own boat.

This dream had at last materialised.

He had a new crew, consisting of men from U-45 and new men who needed nursing. Their working-up period in the Baltic had been brief. Periscope school had been brief. Donitz, desperately anxious to throw everything he had into the Atlantic struggle, committed all. His interview with Wolz had been brief, brilliant, coming straight to the point, like the man himself.

Because Wolz had proved himself capable of command, he would be confirmed in command of U-55. No amount of training could speak so eloquently as a record of success in action.

As for the deadly torpedoes that did not kill – Donitz

12

had instituted a thorough-going investigation. On April 20, the Torpedo Commission had sat to discover why brave men risked their lives to get into firing position and were then badly let down by weapons that did not function.

One result was that the contact pistols, to which the U-boat had reverted, had – at last – begun to sink shipping. All the same, many torpedoes still malfunctioned and ships still sailed to England that should, by rights, if the Gods of War were not so blind, be mouldering on the sea bed.

The scurrying activity around the convoy continued for a space. A ship dropped back. No doubt, reflected Wolz, she was picking up survivors. The destroyers ran and flashed about the flanks, sometimes silhouetted against the dying flames, sometimes just a white bow wave and the hint of a long powerful shape cutting through the water. But, gradually, quietness returned. The blazing patch of oil upon the waters was left astern, dying, dwindling.

The light worsened as cloud built up. After forty minutes Wolz stretched and lifted the voice-pipe cover.

'How are they coming?'

'We have almost completed two, Herr Oberleutnant.'

Wolz made a face, unseen in the darkness.

Two.

The usual time was an hour and a half, a lot less if the men were skilled and conditions perfect. Neitzel knew his theory and had been worked in the academy and the training schools; but when it came right down to working in action, then tension, nerves, fears, sorted the men from the boys.

Wolz cocked his head up, studying the sky.

The overcast was now thickening into a real black vault of cloud. Not a star in sight, the moon vanished, and the darkness clamping down on vision. The lightness of the sky against the sea would help him pick up the silhouettes of the plodding merchantmen; but it would be chancy.

13

'Secure after the second, Herr Leutnant. I shall slip those two in tonight. You can have all day tomorrow to load the other two, as well as the rest.'

'Very good.'

Even through the voice-pipe Wolz heard the scream.

That smashed at him first. It was followed by the clashing rumble, the horrifying clattering clanging as of a steam engine turning over in a tunnel, that told him exactly what had happened.

The screams racketed on and on.

'Take her,' he bellowed at Leutnant Riepold, the Second Officer, on the bridge with him. 'Same course, reduce speed to eight knots.'

Then he was jumping bodily down the ladder through the hatch and raging forrard to the catastrophe in the forward torpedo compartment.

CHAPTER TWO

Jakob Gerhardt had never admitted to his dislike of the dirty and dangerous job of reloading torpedoes at sea. He tried to look at it as just another demand made by the Third Reich upon a loyal member of the Kriegsmarine. But the sight of those long, oily, gleaming cylinders filled him with the kind of dread he had always felt entering the dentist's surgery, so that he had to force himself to work on them.

Hans Leicht, a powerful burly fellow who came from Posen, seemed somehow to guess at this dislike, amounting to fear, that unnerved Gerhardt.

Now they were working in the forward torpedo compartment of U-55 – which was also their mess deck – and the spare eels were being roused out with a consequent disruption of the normal routine of the place.

One tube had already been reloaded.

The men worked in the cramped space on the second reload. The chains, the steel skin of the eel, the spanners and the tools, the bulkheads, everything seemed covered with a slime of water and oil. The pressure popped in a man's ears. That traditional smell of a U-boat compounded of sea-water and pitch and oil and the lingering after-smells of cooking, which could make a haughty battleship man sick to the guts, had no effect on Jakob Gerhardt.

It was just the idea of trying to control over a thousand kilos of dead weight with chains and men's muscles that put him off, chilled him, filled him with forebodings.

Leutnant Neitzel shouted and sweated with the rest of them. The chains were hauled up, the links making that harsh clacking sound. Gingerly, the inert weight was lifted up ready to be pushed forward by main force into the opened rear end of the tube.

Just what happened, Hans Leicht saw with brutal clarity. It is doubtful if Jakob Gerhardt saw anything.

A linkage broke. It pinged across with a musical note very true among the rumbling noise of fans and pumps and the rumble of the diesels, still audible up here in the bows.

Leicht yelled.

Gerhardt screamed.

Leutnant Neitzel was just reporting progress to the skipper.

The only thing Jakob Gerhardt could see was the long gleaming oiled length of the torpedo dropping upon him.

He screamed again as the weight bore him down. His back snapped against a metal ridge, his arms flailed outwards, and the torpedo bore on down on to his ribcage, into his ribcage. That massive weight dragging the useless chains surged across Jakob Gerhardt. The inner cavities of his body were broken open and exposed. His ribs burst out, broken and splintered. His blood gushed,

15

still pumped by a heart that beat for four steady thumpings, sending the red blood spurting in the bright light of the torpedo room. Squashed in, his ribs splayed, his face upturned and his legs kicking spasmodically, Jakob Gerhardt lay trapped beneath the oiled length of the torpedo.

U-55 rolled back gently and the torpedo rolled, smashing away the fittings of the compartment, threatening to tear free of the remaining hoist and charge like an abandoned railway locomotive, tearing everything to destruction.

Leicht hauled himself back to the bulkhead door, yelling.

Leutant Neitzel shouted incoherently.

Men were screaming.

The torpedo twisted and rolled, like a sentient thing, and Waldemar Meyer, a leading torpedo hand, tried to jump aside and was slow.

The torpedo waggled itself and rolled over his foot.

Meyer screamed, and screamed, and went on screaming as he saw his foot crushed, saw the bones splinter, saw the blood gout.

The torpedo compartment was a shambles of yelling men, wildly swinging torpedo and scattered wreckage – and of splashes of bright blood staining the bulkheads, the deck and the faces and bodies of the horrified men.

Baldur Wolz broke into the forward torpedo compartment and checked. His jaw, where already incipient stubble set a golden fuzz about the leanness, thrust forward as he controlled the shock.

He had known what he would see.

But the reality caught at him like an iron fist about his throat. He choked down nausea.

A man hung screaming by the watertight door. It was Hans Leicht, torpedo man.

Wolz slapped him hard across the face, across, back, across.

'Attention! Stop that infernal howling.'

16

Leicht's mouth clacked shut. He half put a hand up, letting go of the door, and then he snapped to attention. He was shaking; and his face looked green; but he stood and he said: 'Very good, Herr Oberleutnant!'

'Leutnant Neitzel!' bellowed Wolz. 'Get this under control instantly!'

The men, as though activated by a spinning motor that released itself the moment the commander rapped out his orders, jumped forward.

Nothing could be done for Jakob Gerhardt.

His body was mashed flat. His head and his legs stuck out either side of the gleaming steel bulk, and his body fluids ran greasily over the steel plating.

'Secure that hoist! Link a chain across! Smartly, now!'

The hands responded. Only one was sick, a young lad from Stade on the Elbe, near Hamburg. His thin shoulders shook as he vomited into a corner. One quick look convinced Wolz that discipline would best be served by letting Jochen spew his guts up out of the way.

The hoist was repaired and the men tailed on.

Slowly, the eel lifted.

The mess stuck. It clung. Gerhardt – well, there were almost two Gerhardts, fore and aft of the gleaming steel cylinder.

'Pass the word for Sanitatsobermaat Reche. Tell him to bring a bucket.'

Neitzel looked distressed at this, as though all the weight of a fractured hoist link would fall on his shoulders, metaphorically only. Literally, the results could be seen smeared over the deck, waiting for Reche and his bucket.

'Herr Leutnant Neitzel! You will oblige me by having the rest of the reloading continued. Report to me the instant you have completed.'

'Very good!'

Wolz turned away.

The relief at leaving the shambles, at not having to look at the obscenely-crushed body of Gerhardt, swept over him. The close smell of the U-boat as he started aft came as a sweetly refreshing breath of Spring air among the Alps after the reek in the forward torpedo compartment.

Because he was Baldur Wolz, because he was the commander of this boat, he made himself stop. He turned around. He went back. He stared at the Third Officer.

'Herr Leutnant Neitzel. I shall require a full written report on the accident. Have it in my cabin by the forenoon watch.'

'Very good, Herr Oberleutnant.'

'Take statements from the men.'

He went out, and this time some sombre mood of prediction made the air in the rest of the U-boat little different from the stench he left.

Leutnant Riepold reported crisply as Wolz climbed the ladder and put his head through the bridge hatch.

The darkness now precluded any further observation of the convoy. U-55 burbled along at eight knots. The attack had begun after midnight, after the stalking into position. The shambles in the torpedo compartment would take time . . .

Wolz made up his mind.

He could easily have acted the big bluff dare-devil and ordered U-55 leaping at eighteen knots over the sea in a courageous and vainglorious hunt for the convoy. But sober calculations told him he'd catch up with the daylight. This was high summer. No. He would nurse his boat during the day and then, tomorrow night, resume the attack.

'Secure from action stations,' he said. 'Keep the same course, Herr Leutnant.'

'Very good.'

The watch would change soon, and then the dawn would come blustering up, bringing with it a little wind. The day should be fine. This summer was proving to be a summer of extraordinarily fine weather. Cousin Manfred had been entirely too convincing about the perfection of

18

the Luftwaffe and this kind of weather would give them the opportunity to batter England to her knees. That, in view of the idiotic stubbornness of the English, seemed in the circumstances the only thing to do with them.

Mind you, there had been something evasive in Manfred's face when the defeat of the British Army had come under excited discussion at one of the innumerable parties at the Schloss. Uncle Siegfried had thrown open house. The gardens and halls and rooms were filled with the brilliance of uniforms. But, on that occasion, Manfred had been reticent. The British had scuttled for home with their tails very firmly between their legs, and to some people, Wolz included, that had appeared a strange business. Why, a fat Major of the Infantry had asked, after the Panzers hauled up, had not the Luftwaffe blown the British to pieces?

Manfred, blond, reckless, waved his glass and bellowed: 'Ask the bomber boys that. We fighters strafed them up, I can tell you. They wouldn't sit down for a week!'

Everyone had laughed and the moment had passed.

All the same, reflected Wolz as he ducked down the hatchway and made his way to the wardroom and his curtained cubby-hole, grandiloquently called his cabin, all the same, it made a simple U-boat man think.

Afterwards, Manfred had referred to the incident, off-handedly, saying in his casual way: 'He's in the infantry and he's fat. Well, I mean to say, Baldur old fellow – that tells you all you need to know, doesn't it?'

And Wolz had nodded and said: 'I suppose so.'

Despite the calamity that had struck with such brutal force in the forward torpedo compartment, the feeling of well-being, of a wonderful sense that he was at last entering upon his rightful kingdom, continued to bubble like his uncle's best champagne. To command his very own boat! He had been lucky. No use denying it. But for the chance that U-55 had been shelled by those devilish English destroyers and gone aground and been abandoned by her crew, he would not be here now. He had left that idiot Forstner fuming on the runway as the aircraft took off for Narvik. He had salved the boat and brought her back to Germany, not without an adventure or two on the way.

He might still be struggling under an almost intolerable burden as second in command to Forstner. That, he knew now and with sober intensity, would have driven him mad after another cruise. Forstner was not almost intolerable; he *was* intolerable.

Once again Wolz refused to think of what had subsequently occurred with the die-hard Party member.

He lay on his bunk, not sleeping, but working out in his mind the relative courses of convoy and U-55.

The British would make their usual change of course after an attack. But here, drawing ever closer to England, their alternatives were narrowing down. The chart of the Atlantic rose in his mind. Yes, by turning to the northeast just before dawn he ought to be in a good position.

During the next routine report to BdU he would have to tell them of the accident in the torpedo room and this would explain his reason for breaking off the action.

But, and the warm glow began and spread; but, he had done very well.

The tanker, according to the book, was of eight thousand tons. The two freighters between them mustered only four thousand two hundred. So, in his first patrol, he had already notched up twelve thousand two hundred.

Then his face creased so that the lines around his mouth stretched.

That should really be eight thousand two hundred and fifty – if you counted the garbage scow.

But Baldur Wolz preferred not to count that.

He still felt that annoying mixture of acute embarrassment, futile anger and wholly enjoyable amusement at the incident.

Ehrenberger, his Number One, would mention it from time to time, a little proudly, as though the name U-55 had earned for herself in the U-boat arm was not one to

20

make a commanding officer throw his hat to the deck and jump on it.

It would not be right to check the forward compartment until the place had been put to order. He wanted to run his boat according to the rules; but he was totally aware that the rules he followed would be the rules as laid down by Oberleutnant z. S. Baldur Wolz.

He was up on the bridge well before dawn, peering into the north east, willing the distant specks of the convoy to break in steady succession over the horizon.

With the brightening of the light a strict and continuous lookout concentrated on the north-east.

Wolz fretted.

The day dawned, clear and with most of the overnight cloud blown away by the wind he had felt in his bones. The sea tumbled about them, running, alive, filled with the early-morning tints of colour, which gave a lustre to the grey-green Atlantic rollers.

But there was no sign of the convoy.

There was no use cursing.

No matter what course he had steered, apart from staying in contact, none would have given him absolute assurance of a regained contact, and the worry over the neglect of the other two boats to attack persisted. One or another of them should be calling up now to report progress. BdU would collate all the various reports and sightings and base their tactics for the night on their best appreciation of the situation.

Perhaps, Wolz conceded, perhaps he should have tried to stick closer to the convoy all night. But – and despite all he felt this keenly – but he had been practically toothless. The wildly gyrating torpedo would have prevented any work from going on in the forward torpedo compartment. He still had his stern tube.

All the same, as close in as he had been to the convoy – and closer still as it would have been necessary for him to maintain contact during those dark hours – would have brought a destroyer on to him. A normal routine sweep around the flanks of the convoy would have brought the Englishman stumbling across him. Toothless, except for the difficult stern-shot, he would have been a sitting duck after the first exchange.

He might have eluded the destroyer easily underwater; he might not. That was a fox and hounds game to be played out to a finish one of these days.

He felt he had chosen the safest course. He hoped it was the wisest. Certainly it was not the way one of your dare-devil press-on skippers of U-boats would have chosen. But Wolz thought of the well-being of the crew, the truth that there would be another convoy along, when he would be in fighting shape to take a full toll. Maybe he hadn't done what a real aces-high, top-notch killer of a U-boat ace would have done; but the trouble was, that type so often never returned from patrol.

And he was on his way. He had twelve thousand two hundred tons to prove it.

When the radio shack sizzled and crackled and the signals flew from U-55 and back from BdU, the pink flimsy handed to him contained instructions to proceed west. A convoy had been picked up. This convoy was important and was following in the tracks of the convoy Wolz had attacked in the night, hoping to be shielded as by a broom sweeping the seas clean before it.

Ehrenberger lifted an eyebrow.

'That's right, Kern,' said Wolz. 'We rendezvous with the pack and then, the night after tonight, we attack. This time I want every eel to work. Every last one.'

Already he had his eye on that fifty thousand ton mark.

U-55 turned her sharp bows into the west and worked up to cruising speed, her grey shape sliding through the seas like a great steel shark.

CHAPTER THREE

Captain Louis Augier, master of the S.S. *Belphegor*, was not a happy man. As far as he had been able to make out from the New York papers, and the Canadian authorities, the war was over. Yet, here he was, sailing his venerable vessel back to England in company with a motley collection of vessels of various nationalities, across a hostile sea swarming with deadly submarines.

Louis Augier possessed a stomach, and a thatch of dark hair, and an eye very piercing, which he was accustomed to use with great effect on pretty women – and on sailors who were foolish enough to sign on under his command. His small beard gave him, he fancied, a dapper air, and mitigated to some extent the deplorable effect of his stomach. But Augier liked the good things of life too much to concern himself over his protuberance; the pretty women did not seem to mind.

As *Belphegor* steamed on towards England, Augier fancied that in the female department, at any rate, his luck had smiled on him. There were these nurses. French girls who had been in America or Canada, and who were now anxious to return to nurse the wounded in this senseless continuing war.

Of course, it was all the fault of the rogue Churchill and this madman de Gaulle. Who was this General de Gaulle, anyway? Augier had never heard of him before. And now, here he was, lean and lanky, with a nose, talking about the Free French, and promising years more of bloodshed.

So Augier gave a little attention to seeing that his First Mate kept the old *Belphegor* somewhere in the station allotted to him in the convoy, and turned the full battery of those piercing eyes on his pretty passengers.

He had made a number of eminently satisfying conquests. The ladies were in need of comfort and reassurance. But the prize of them all, this young, contemptuous, icy Mademoiselle Angelique Savinien, rebuffed him with such an air of indifference as positively to infuriate him, and render extraordinarily hot those portions of his anatomy he considered his most powerful assets.

Belphegor plugged along, and drew upon herself more than one irate signal from the convoy commodore. She strayed from her position. She made too much smoke. She must be more careful about the refuse tipped over her side . . .

'Ma foi!' declared Augier. 'Am I then a refuse barge to store rotting cabbage on my decks?'

The First Mate, a thick-set, gorilla-like man who had found a thin, spiky, angular lady who was amenable to trying her rudimentary first-aid upon him, shrugged his shoulders with resignation, and vented his captain's spleen upon the crew.

So S.S. *Belphegor* plunged and waltzed and wriggled her way across the Atlantic.

The convoy had been met at last by the homeward bound escort. This consisted of an ancient V and W class destroyer converted for long-range escort work, two of the new little corvettes, and a trawler who, whilst she could keep the sea at times when other vessels must run for it, was of small capacity in the fight against the U-boat. But she would serve her part, and valiantly.

This trawler, *Maggie Dee*, cavorted about the convoy like a puppy with a slipper. Even the two corvettes, H.M.S. *Nemesia* and *Aquilegia*, gave an appearance of bulkiness beside her. As for the V and W class, H.M.S. *Vagrant*, she still retained her lean low wolfish look of the hunter.

On these four vessels rested the safe-keeping of forty-one ships.

The four escorts picked up the inward-bound convoy, spent some time in sorting out the lines, and then settled

24

down to their task of battling through the iron ring of U-boats they knew Admiral Donitz would throw about them – if they were sighted.

U-55 steamed west on the surface, her diesels rumbling with the steady, reassuring note that Wolz always associated with the expert ministrations of Loeffler. Not that the engine-room crew were slouches; with the Engineer Officer to chase their backsides they were turning into a reliable bunch. But the training sessions had been short. Donitz was desperately short of U-boats. The losses so far sustained and the new additions to the underwater fleet exactly balanced out. If the war was to be won – all over again, as Wolz saw it, remembering the excited talk of his friends at home – then a vast number of boats had to be sent out on patrol to sink English ships.

He spent a great deal of time on the bridge, wedged into his corner, his glasses handy.

The lookouts had to be trusted. But he was still new enough in command to want to be everywhere at once.

As to his officers, Ehrenberger was first class, a good man and a comrade. Riepold, who had served in U-55 before and had stuck with her during the period when she had been beached, promised in his meticulous, by-the-book way to prove of value. It was on the third officer, Leutnant zur See Neitzel, that Baldur Wolz pondered most often.

The feldwebels and the unteroffiziers would be sorted out; already he was dividing them up in his mind, and he would take the earliest and most ruthless opportunity of getting rid of those he felt were unreliable. He had considered himself lucky in getting Lindner. The cox'n had spent a long and – not from what he said but from his expression and the look in his eyes – rapturous leave with his bride. If thoughts of home might weaken a man during the harsh and brutal necessities of life at sea, Hans Lindner gave no sign that home sickness affected him. He was, Wolz felt sure, as much committed to this stuggle for the Fatherland as he was himself, detesting war but convinced that the only way Germany could hold up her head, proudly and with confidence, lay in convincing the world she was once more a great power.

If the decadent democracies did not like that, then they must take the consequences.

France had already gone.

How the news had thrilled them all!

The uproar and the celebrations had continued interminably. Uncle Siegfried, whilst expressing his satisfaction that the French were on the receiving end this time, had also indicated that some of the contracts he had been confidently expecting for war materials might not now materialise. He was rich enough, he said, and so that aspect of it all did not upset him as much as it might another. Lottie, who was a friend of the family, said that her father, who was not quite as rich and not quite as grand as Uncle Siegfried, was more worried than he admitted. But, all the same, what concerned Uncle Siegfried was the continued intransigence of England.

'After all, Baldur,' he said, as he prepared to take himself off to Berlin for another of the conferences that absorbed so much of his time. 'With France gone, what hope is there for England? You know the English, Baldur, what do you have to say?'

The schloss was particularly attractive that year, the gardens superb with colour, the trees of a brilliant summer green that he knew he would remember with great nostalgia when the grey seas lashed over the casing and splattered him with foam.

'The English?' said Wolz. He remembered the green of English trees, the summer sun over English lawns, and the racial ritual of cricket. He had made friends there. There had been pranks, fantastically stupid larks. He remembered with particular affection Sub-lieutenant Richard Algernon Mitchell. That maniac with his M.G. and his flannel bags and his never-ending procession of girl friends might have been a good German, as Wolz saw it, one of the energetic crowd who filled the schloss with noise and clamour. Wolz fancied his three cousins

26

would get on with Mitchell, particularly Manfred, the Luftwaffe pilot. Cousin Siegfried might have a few reservations; after all, Siegfried was SS and therefore a cut above most other people in his own estimation. As for Cousin Helmut, Wolz was now more certain than ever that Helmut was Gestapo. But, for all that, Helmut remained friendly to his cousin Baldur Wolz and the family got along as well as they always had.

His uncle fussed with an attaché case over-stuffed with papers. He went towards the entrance and the steps on to the gravel drive where the long, highly-polished black Mercedes waited.

'Yes, Baldur. The English. Are they really all fools? or just mad?'

'Most of the ones I know were mad. That seemed to be so. They did some foolish things. But fools?'

The sunshine warmed as they went down the steps to the Mercedes.

'They have been tricked by this villain Churchill. He will be the first to be shot, you mark me, Baldur.'

'I suppose so. But I can't think of them as fools. Silly, soft, uncaring, yes.'

'The war has been won. But they don't seem to understand that.'

Wolz could not stop himself from blurting out: 'They have a saying there, about losing all the battles except the last one.'

'Humph! I have heard that before. They talk of Waterloo. Did you ask them who won Waterloo, Baldur? And did they say their famous Iron Duke? All the world knows Waterloo was won by Blucher. We won Waterloo, just as we won the battle they call Jutland.'

Wolz would not be drawn into that old argument again.

He saw his uncle off for Berlin and went back up the steps. Cousin Siegfried was due this evening, and if he went according to form he would be bringing Marlene

27

with him. Wolz had ambivalent feelings about the exotic Marlene.

A distant roaring in the air, a trembling note that set a throbbing chiming in his head, heralded the swift passage overhead of a gruppe of Heinkel He 111s. The thirty twin-engined planes flew in perfect formation. Tilting his head back, one foot on the top step, Wolz watched them.

They made a brave sight, a reassuring sight. The idea of being in the uniform of a Polish or French or British soldier and seeing that fast-moving, heavily-armed gruppe of aeroplanes diving on him was one that did not appeal in the slightest to Baldur Wolz, an idea that made him realise even more strongly how fortunate any man was in these days to be German.

The black crosses on the wings gleamed brightly.

Wolz did not wave.

As he went back into the schloss he could not stop himself from wondering again just how it could happen that the British Army could escape. Mind you, there had been so few of them left that, to all intents and purposes, they had been totally destroyed. He had studied the pictures in *Signal* and felt a warm satisfaction at the complete victory won by the forces of the Third Reich.

Pictures of Panzers storming forward, of burning towns and gutted cities – one picture of Rotterdam indicated graphically the results of aerial bombing – pictures of exhausted and disillusioned Tommies, pictures, too, of the sub-human people the French Empire recruited into the ranks of its now-shattered army, spoke eloquently of what had happened.

The war had been won.

And those idiotic Englishmen insisted on going on with the struggle that for them was utterly useless.

Sub-lieutenant Dick Mitchell would be in the fight. Suddenly, Wolz realised that Dick Mitchell wouldn't give a damn. He must be a lieutenant by now, possibly a lieutenant-commander if things had gone well for him. Wolz's own promotion to Kapitanleutnant could not now be long delayed. Of course, Dick Mitchell – whom those who did not know him very well called Ram Mitchell – might already be dead.

That reflection struck Wolz shrewdly on two levels. His first instinctive reaction was one of sorrow. Dick Mitchell was, as his English friends said, a good egg. He'd talked on about submarines and expected to be posted to destroyers. Yes, if he was already killed in the war Wolz would be sad. But, against that, the sombre knowledge that Mitchell was an enemy, a man he must welcome dead in war, chilled him. The two feelings strove, one with the other.

The schloss echoed with noise and laughter one moment and the next was chill and silent. There was a deal of coming and going. Lottie telephoned in a tremendous rush and asked if he could meet her at the station. She was going straight through; but, she said in her breathy voice fluttering against his eardrum through the receiver, but there would be time.

At the station the hustle and bustle of wartime Germany unlimbering after a successful war struck Wolz as odd, and premature. Lottie's train steamed wheezily to itself. There would be a wait of thirty minutes, she told him.

She looked her usual pert self, ravishing in a long jersey with a tight belt. Her high heels were high. Her legs – Wolz knew all about those slender, tapering legs.

'Oh, Baldur! So you came!'

'And I'm here to prove it.'

She was demurely made-up, as was proper; but he saw a desperateness in the sparkle of her. Her hair had been freshly set and, privately, he felt it did not suit her. Her face looked thinner than it should be. But, for all that, she was still alluring in her breezy, laughing, careless way.

'I'm sharing this compartment with a couple who have five children – all spoiled brats. And there is a rather nice Panzer leutnant – his pink collar-edging is so . . . so . . .'

She was trying to work her way up to telling him something.

'And there are two Berlin businessmen who talk about getting back into production now the war is over –'

'Almost over.'

'Yes?' She looked at him uncertainly. 'I suppose so. They have all gone to the refreshment room and we have twenty minutes alone together.' She rose, a lithe, sinuous movement, and pulled down the blind on the window by her shoulder.

'What's the trouble, Lottie? Your father?'

She leaned forward and pulled the next blind down.

'Since mother died he's grown tired, very tired. And he doesn't seem able to pull in the contracts like he used to.'

'You heard those businessmen. We're able to make a few domestic things now, instead of tanks and guns. Butter –'

'Yes.'

'Tell me, lovey. If I can help –'

'Only in one way, Baldur. I think I might have to marry some red-necked fat oaf in a munitions plant – something to do with bringing the two families together. Father is worn out.'

She lifted her skirt and, quite matter-of-factly, pulled her knickers down. She wadded them up and, instead of throwing them at Wolz's head, placed them carefully in her bag. She moved delicately, deliberately.

'Lottie!'

'If you hang about the time will be gone. No one can see from the station and there are only tracks on the other side.'

She plumped herself down on the seat at his side and began to pull at his buttons. Wolz laughed, letting her get on with it. He pulled her skirt up over her thighs as far as it would go against the railway compartment seat. She wore her knickers over the silk-stocking suspender straps. The dark stocking tops looked remarkably alluring against her skin, rounded and warm and firm. He stroked the tips of his fingers over her thighs.

30

'You know, Baldur. If I do have to get married, I don't know what I shall do with you.'

'And, suppose I marry?' Lottie had no idea – as, indeed, had no one apart from the two of them – how far his feelings for Trudi von Hartstein were leading him. Marriage was a very strong possibility there. Lottie's legs were lovely. 'And if we're both married?'

She had the buttons undone now and Wolz shifted around to help her. She let the tip of her tongue moisten her lips.

'So we get married. Hurry up, Baldur! I've been as dry as the Sahara these past months!'

He put his hand to her cheek and tilted her head and kissed her. The heat of her mouth stormed at him, her tongue a darting flame against his. Her hands were all over him, and he responded, urgent now, not giving a damn if the door did open and the Station Master poked his head in. He had his own demands on him now.

Lottie groaned and half-stood, then she sat down on him. He clasped her around the waist, burying his face between her breasts. She rocked.

Eventually, when they were tidy, she said: 'I'm glad you came, Baldur.'

And he said: 'So am I.'

Rousing himself from his corner of the bridge of U-55 Wolz accepted the cup of coffee brought up to the conning tower. The day glittered brightly about him; U-55 sailed like a dream, the steady thrum of her exhausts music in the ears. The men could get themselves dry and the evils of heat and cold, twin devils that plagued a U-boat man, could for the moment be forgotten.

Routine continued. The food supplies, so carefully packed away in the narrow pressure hull of the boat so that the stuff needing to be eaten first was packed last, yielded still fine meals. They were provisioned in royal style, as they ought to be. Now, even more than before the debacle that had overtaken France, if England was to be knocked out, then the U-boats would do it.

But Wolz was well aware that many people did not share that opinion. The U-boat arm was sadly depleted, or, rather, unable to put forward any real show of strength. Manfred, filled with the gusto and the deviltry of the Luftwaffe, was confident that England would not survive direct attack. Siegfried, too, contented himself with saying that once the Panzers landed at Brighton or Hastings or Dover, the English would collapse.

Wolz, at sea in his own U-boat, insisted to himself that all that made no difference. His job, for which he had been trained and to which he was dedicated by an unshaken belief in the justice of his cause, was to sink English ships.

On the afternoon of the following day they picked up the first of their companion U-boats of the gathering pack – and made the first sighting of the convoy.

CHAPTER FOUR

The broad rectangle of the convoy spread across the ocean. Their formation was a mess; but to Commodore John Horning, who had once been a Vice-Admiral on active duty and was now working on duty far more vital than ever he had seen wearing his admiral's flag, the formation was as good as he could hope to achieve. He had sailed from Newfoundland with forty-two ships and, rather to his surprise, he still had forty-one in company. They had, so far, not been attacked. The lost loner had simply disappeared one morning and not been seen again. Probably, either with engine trouble of some kind or another, or with a skipper who just did not like convoys, she was straggling along on her own to the rear.

For whatever reason she straggled, she was in Horning's eyes a dead duck.

A tall, spare man with tufty eyebrows and a lean nose, his eyes deeply sunk and the lines in his face etched by years of fighting the ocean weather all around the globe, Horning often wondered what on earth had induced him to come back to sea to shepherd a flock of bloody-minded merchant skippers and their unwieldy charges about the Atlantic. But the work was vital and he was proud to be given the chance when he was past sixty.

His Yeoman of signals, Weatherby, was a solid York-shireman, and shared his commodore's disgust at the antics of the sailors under the Red Ensign.

Their only escort from Newfoundland had been the Armed Merchant Cruiser H.M.S. *Archon*, a thirteen thousand five hundred tonner armed with a few paltry six-inch guns that had seen better days. Against U-boats she would be of no more use than any one of the merchant ships in convoy. Against a German pocket battle-ship or battlecruiser, she would be helplessly overmatched – the gallant example of *Rawalpindi* showed that with awful clarity.

Now the close escort had joined, Horning felt only marginally better. True, he had a destroyer, two sloops and a trawler, in these straightened days after Dunkirk an escort of some strength compared with the convoys that had run in with a single sloop or corvette alone. But he had no illusions left. They must steam on doggedly and hope to bring in at least some of the convoy. That they would lose ships if the U-boats sighted them was inevitable.

H.M.S. *Vagrant* foamed along ahead, cutting a course across the convoy, weaving back to patrol the windward side. The two corvettes covered the flanks. The trawler, *Maggie Dee*, plunged along astern, already half-smothered with spray even in this easy sea and at this leisurely speed.

3   33

Archon towered in the centre of the formation. She sailed to starboard of the commodore's flagship, S.S. *Crampton*, with the flags and the halyards and the appurtenances of that signalling system that he used so vehemently to keep the ships in station and emitting as little smoke as possible.

The confounded Frenchman was always in trouble.

Belphegor lurched along, apparently trying to ram her next ahead, then, in the next moment, trying to get herself rammed by her next astern. She belched black smoke every now and then and brought down the wrath of Horning and the quick flurried visit of a corvette, with the *whyup! whyup!* to remind her of her naughty ways.

The Frenchman remained indifferent to signals, and just plugged along as though he sailed the ocean alone.

Giving another long look around the horizon, a look of anxiety and awareness of imminent peril, Horning went back into the sea cabin to find his steward with a cup of kai and a smile.

Well, at times like these it was not all hell at sea.

But these times came rarely, and would disappear altogether once the wolf pack caught them in its iron jaws.

Three U-boats rode the long gentle swell together under the afternoon sun.

This calm, almost casual meeting of boats out in the broad wastes of the Atlantic never failed to move Wolz. He gazed on the lean shapes of the other boats with real affection and pride. He was the junior boy, and even though once an attack had commenced each commander was strictly on his own, he must in the initial stages come under command of the senior officer.

The fourth and fifth boats had radioed they were on their way from a point to the south and expected to join before midnight.

As the sun sank and flooded the sea with orange and ochre tints, lambent against the long running swell of the sea, Wolz stared hungrily out to the horizon.

The convoy had been kept in contact.

This was the night he notched up more kills, added to the total slowly accumulating, perhaps gained for himself that coveted first fifty thousand tons. It was not, given a little luck and determination, impossible.

The imponderable remained the performance of the torpedoes.

Those tricky eels could rob him of deserved victory.

Ehrenberger voiced similar doubts, and Wolz felt he had to say, smartly: 'Brace up, Kern! We have a good boat, Loeffler sees to that. We have checked and rechecked the eels. Tonight, we go in and sink!'

This night the moon was sufficient for them to go downmoon and attack from the port side of the convoy, with the ships silhouetted against the light upmoon of them.

Chugging along on diesels, brazenly on the surface, Wolz took U-55 in.

According to the rough plan worked out between the commanders, U-55 stalked up on the port bow, moving just fast enough to gain position, and not so fast that she would throw up a betraying bow wave.

Wolz gripped the coaming of the bridge and stared as the hazy light of the moon danced across the water. He could see the black distant silhouettes of the British ships draw closer. Every now and then he gave a low-voiced order to the helmsman. U-55 responded perfectly. The convoy came closer and closer.

Searching very carefully, Wolz picked out the mass of shipping, seeing tankers and freighters, the towering superstructure of a liner – wait a minute! That would be an Armed Merchant Cruiser! He'd had a brush with one of these before, after the fiasco of the River Plate cruise.

In his own mind the first targets must be tankers, ammunition ships, freighters. Perhaps, if she came into his sights and presented herself, he'd loose at the A.M.C. Not otherwise.

'Destroyer!' sang out the starboard stern lookout. Then: 'Coming up fast on the starboard beam.'

Wolz swung to look.

They were still far enough from the port column. The destroyer would pass between them and the convoy. Wolz picked her up instantly. She was not travelling all that fast – he made a mental note to check the lookout after the battle. It was young Johann Henke, one of the two midshipmen assigned U-55, and he was keen as mustard.

'That fellow won't see us,' said Wolz, making his voice hard and confident. 'We'll just let him hustle by.'

The escort swung past up the flank of the convoy.

The moment their converging course had intersected and opened out again, Wolz took U-55 in once more. The massed ranks of ships and the U-boats were two imponderable weights, clashing together, ready to fill the night with fire and blood and violence.

'Switch in, Kern. Mind you hit them clean.'

The periscope and the attack table were coupled in. Wolz conned U-55 nearer. The sea washed across the forward casing and around the 8.8 centimetre; but at their speed no betraying breaking suds boiled up around the gun or conning tower. Almost invisibly they ghosted in.

Wolz made his decisions.

The destroyer was now invisible ahead; she must have gone around the front of the convoy. He made a careful sweep with the glasses down the port flank of the convoy and could make out no hostile shape of an escort. Now was the chance.

The boat moved smoothly through the swell. Ahead in the port column loomed the bulk of a freighter. He could see no tankers near and that was normal; valuable or vulnerable ships would be positioned near to the centre of the convoy.

Four tubes, four torpedoes, four ships.

He made his four targets and passed them to Ehrenberger.

The bows of the boat swung.

The soft voices called off the ranges and the angles.

36

Then –
'Loose!'

The torpedo that smashed into S.S. *Harpel* ripped apart the plating over her boiler room, deluged the entire compartment with tons of water, tore her practically in half. She went down in little over a minute.

Only ten men survived that first horrific blast.

As the ship, broken into two raking halves pointing at the sky, slid below the surface, water bubbled and broke, the expected explosion smashed upwards, completing the tale of destruction.

Only four men were left clinging to a hatch cover.

Nemesia swung across to the port column where the explosions had occurred. Her captain, Lieutenant Commander Dunton, had taken his ship to sea for the first time in earnest just six weeks before. His crew were green, he was an R.N.R. officer with no first-hand experience of the horrendous conditions of the Western Approaches.

He stopped to lower a boat to pick up survivors and then, taking what he considered to be the likely track of the torpedo as a guide, raced off at his best speed, something around fourteen knots, to investigate.

'Good God!' shouted Dunton, as his ears and eyes were assaulted by the blast from over his right shoulder. He swung about, shocked. *Nemesia* shook and leaped to the titanic explosion.

A ship in the fifth column had gone up in a single fantastic ball of fire.

Black against the moonlight the gyrating column of mushrooming smoke burst upwards from the remnants of the ship.

'Ammunition ship,' said his Number One. They both stared, feeling sick.

Nemesia ran out to port for half a mile; but nothing was seen.

When further explosions erupted from the convoy, coming from the stern, Dunton swung his corvette about and hared off there, shaking, hoping to find at least some sign of the bastards who were tearing the convoy to pieces.

Three other ships were ripped apart. Two sank quickly; the third continued afloat, and men were clinging to the burning hull, waiting for some miracle to save them.

Aquilegia ran alongside; but before anything could be done, the ship slowly turned over.

Screaming men were pitchforked into the sea.

Lieutenant-Commander Raymond gave what orders he could.

'But there's nothing we can do, Number One, save stand by and pick up survivors.'

'There's nothing on asdic, sir,' said his Number One.

'Tell the lookouts to keep their eyes peeled.'

'Very difficult to pick up a U-boat, sir.'

'You don't have to tell me!' flared Raymond. He hunched into his collar and turned away. The feeling of helplessness tore at a man, made him feel the uselessness of it all.

When a torpedo claimed a tanker and the sea became covered with burning oil the horror mounted to a crescendo.

Men covered in oil were burning in the sea.

Hands, faces, bare chests, all were burning, frizzling, frying.

A few survivors were hauled in over the side.

The sight of these men, half-naked, burned, dying, wounded, struck deeply into the mind of Lieutenant-Commander Raymond. He watched as they were taken below. He wondered how many of them, if any, would survive.

And still the slaughter went on.

Captain Louis Augier saw the explosions. He saw the ammunition ship erupt in a single awesome fountain of destruction.

Belphegor passed a group of men in the water, all dead, aimlessly swirling in the wake of the ship's passage.

His head felt as though it would burst.

His protuberant stomach made deep bubbling noises.

He clutched the rail of the bridge wing and stared in horror upon the corpses lolling in the water, upheld by their life jackets, and he touched his own life jacket and shuddered.

'Has not Marshal Petain concluded peace with the Germans?' he suddenly shouted at the quartermaster, turning to run into the wheel house. 'Why do they try to kill us?'

A deep thud smashed against the plating of *Belphegor*. The ship shook.

Augier was thrown to his knees. He lifted a distraught face, shaking, weeping, his hands clawing in a vain attempt to protect himself from the German torpedoes.

'We have been torpedoed!' he screamed.

But the quartermaster was gone and the wheel spun idly.

He understood the meaning of that savage and menacing thump.

In any second the old *Belphegor* would turn turtle, would explode, would rip apart, and the sea would come pouring in.

With the others of the crew, shouting, yelling, fighting, the quartermaster roared at the davits to swing the boats out.

Helping along in the confusing darkness, blackened even more as smoke from burning ships obscured the moonlight, the nurses clustered together, waiting to enter the boats pointed out to them as theirs. The women remained calm in the confusion.

Belphegor began to list. The list was slow and steady; but it struck fresh panic among men already unsure, uncertain, unaware of what was to happen to them.

The boats were lowered with commendable speed.

Men and woman began to leave the ship, and, with a grace that Captain Augier profoundly gave thanks for, not a single lifeboat capsized.

They pulled away into the flame-shot darkness, with

a hint of the moonlight showing around the roiling edges of the black clouds of destruction. The sea remained calm.

Presently, *Maggie Dee* came up and took them aboard.

When *Belphegor* shuddered and groaned and the uproar began on deck, Angelique Savinien knew at once what had happened.

She scrambled from the bunk placed at her disposal in the small cabin she shared with three other girls going to England to become nurses. The call by General de Gaulle had found her in Canada, where she was visiting her mother's sister. Her aunt had invited her in those ominous days of August 1939, and she had gone with all the excitement of any eighteen-year-old.

Now, now that her beloved France had fallen and the call had been sent, she was on her way back to do her duty.

Only, only it looked very much as though she might never make the first part of the journey.

'Quickly, Marie!' she cried. 'We must go up on deck.'

The girls might have screamed in fear, but Angelique bustled them out of the cabin. She made them take up warm jackets. The door slid along its runners, idly, and slid back, the fastening hanging loose.

They burst into the passageway and made for the companionway leading on to the boat deck. A mass of men, all shouting and swearing, were swinging the boats out.

The ship listed a little; but Angelique, who knew nothing of large boats, and a little of dinghy sailing with her cousins in Quebec, felt the tilt terribly.

The ladies conducting the would-be nurses to England remained calm, and that heartened Angelique.

Marie, a slight, fluffy blonde girl, was crying quietly to herself, and trembling. Angelique put her pretty jacket more firmly around her shoulders, trying to comfort her.

'It is my crucifix, Angelique. I left it under my pillow.'

Angelique looked at the boats being swung out. It would take perhaps four minutes for her to run back and fetch the little cross. Marie would be inconsolable.

'Stay with madame!' cautioned Angelique. 'You know your boat, number two. I am in number four, so if I do not see you immediately, I will give you your cross when we are rescued.'

'But, Angelique –'

But Angelique Savinien was gone.

She was accustomed to making decisions, having to cope with three younger brothers. She was a tall girl, well-formed, with a narrow waist and firm breasts. Her legs were so long, she had often ruefully said, that stockings were going to be a perennial problem. Her hair, of a lustrous darkness, and the oval face with the large soft brown eyes, were just calculated to make men turn their heads, and whistle.

She always tossed her own head in disdain.

Men! That terrible captain! What an old goat he was! She suspected that madame knew the inside of the captain's cabin rather better than she should.

Belphegor groaned and heaved in the water as Angelique reached the cabin. The lights still glowed dimly; but as she reached under the pillow and her hand closed on Marie's cross, the lights went out.

Darkness closed in.

Instantly, Angelique bit down on her automatic cry.

She could find her way back easily enough, by trailing a hand along the passage on the brass rail. The stairs were there, and she had only to run up them and be back where the boats were being lowered.

The old ship – she had been built in Marseilles too many years ago to count – lurched again. She had not entirely lost steerage way and from the rumble of the engines they were still turning. Angelique turned back and felt her way across to the cabin door.

It was shut.

She took hold of the handle and pulled.

The door did not slide along its runners.

41

She took a good grip, braced herself, and heaved.

The door did not move.

A nasty taste of bile entered her mouth. She found she was breathing very quickly. Her head hurt.

Once again she heaved at the door.

It would not budge a millimetre.

Suddenly she was sobbing and crying, beating at the door with her closed fists, shrieking.

Faintly she could hear the noises overhead, strange rumbles and creakings, a thin shrieking she thought was a woman screaming and then realised from its continuous note that it must be the falls running through ungreased sheaves.

She banged and kicked the door and hurt her hands and her toes. Presently she could not hear any noises from above save the usual ship noises all about her.

In the darkness, Angelique Savinien sank to her knees beside the prison door, too frightened to cry, too scared to do anything but huddle there and wait for what must come.

CHAPTER FIVE

'They call themselves escorts,' exclaimed Baldur Wolz. 'But they are like blind old women trying to cross the road. They see nothing!'

'They fire enough star shells,' observed Ehrenberger.

He had come on to the bridge with Wolz and the look-outs. It was vital to keep the number of personnel on the bridge down to the absolute minimum. At one-and-a fifth seconds for each man to hurl himself headlong down the conning tower hatch, and the diving time of a U-boat set as much lower than fifty seconds, as a smart commander could make it, the calculations were obvious.

More than once Wolz, as last down, had descended in a spray of spouting white water.

Bending to the voice pipe, Wolz gave a course correction to the helmsman. To the torpedo compartment forward – a compartment that would not contain horrific memories for him – he said: 'Nearly finished?'

'Almost, Herr Oberleutnant.'

Leutnant Neitzel had again been entrusted with the reloading job. Wolz could have left it to the torpedo petty officer; but Neitzel had to learn what life was like. In the U-boats lay a hard, a very hard, school.

'And how long is almost, Herr Leutnant?'

A sound somewhere between a cough and a grunt at the other end of the line indicated Neitzel understood, and did not care for, his skipper's rebuke.

'Ten minutes, Herr Oberleutnant.'

'Make it so.'

Wolz went back to stare upon the fantastic scene spread all across the horizon.

Ships burned.

The scurrying black silhouettes of ships passed between the bonfires. Every now and then an explosion and a gush of flame-irradiated smoke would indicate the end of another ship. Wolz knew he had sunk two – two of the damned eels had misbehaved again – and there were another five or six going down. This was the way to throttle England's lifeline.

As for the colossal explosion of the ammunition ship going up, that had lifted them from the deck, plastered their eyelids against their eyeballs, nearly deafened them. The concussion had rocked and shaken U-55 like a terrier-gripped rat.

Baldur Wolz found he did not much care for that image. Far more vivid was the image of a savage beast of the jungle stalking game at the water hole.

There were unpleasant after-effects of the mammoth explosion which Loeffler reported.

43

Wolz went down the conning tower ladder in a foul mood. Only moments before he had been feeling on top of the world, even prepared – almost – to forgive the malfunction of the two torpedoes. He was not prepared to admit he had missed. He could have done, of course; but they had been dead on, everything right, and had hit with two.

The one that had taken the ammunition ship had also been one that might, all things considered, have been one that had failed, instead of the one, say, aimed at the very large freighter near her.

'It doesn't look too good, skipper.'

Loeffler had easily fallen into calling Wolz skipper. There might have been an awkwardness to be expected; but it flowed naturally, and, even, in quiet or raucous off-duty hours, Loeffler would call him Baldur to his own Kurt.

In the confined space of the engine room, Wolz bent to look. He admitted with perfect frankness that he did not know anything like as much about the engines as did Loeffler; but he knew enough. Engines and the machinery of the U-boat were Loeffler's department; but Wolz knew enough.

'I see.' He straightened to his usual half-crouch in this cramped space. 'The crack is there, without doubt.'

The crankshaft had been so firmly nudged by the munitions ship that it had incontinently cracked. The split was a hairline fracture at the moment; but the starboard engine could not be run at anything like full revolutions.

'If you did run her, skipper, I'm not guaranteeing any life time. We are effectively on one engine.'

'Is there any other damage?'

'If there is, I'll get to it. This beauty was the first one I ran across. But, skipper, and not to look too much on the black side, there will be more, yes?'

Loeffler's pugnacious, flat-nosed, red-bearded face gleamed in the harsh lighting. He looked annoyed, as he rightly deserved to be. His cherished engines had been

44

knocked about and he didn't like it.

Neither did Wolz.

'I'm going to attack the moment the reloads are in. Give me the speed you can, Kurt. If we crack the shaft we crack it. But I must have speed at the right moment.'

Loeffler wiped his hands on the inevitable scrap of waste.

'You mean the wrong moment, don't you, skipper?'

'Yes,' Wolz nodded. 'I suppose I do.'

Because of the confusion in the forward mess decks consequent upon the reloading, Waldemar Meyer had been shifted, temporarily. Wolz looked in on him.

'You feeling more comfortable, Meyer?'

'Yes, skipper, thank you.'

'Reche seems to think you'll be able to walk again. You lost four toes, was it?'

'Three, skipper.'

'Three! Well, there you are. Your luck was in.'

Wolz did not miss Meyer's expression in the merciless lighting; shock and then resentment and then – acceptance.

And it was true.

He was back on the bridge when Neitzel rang through to report the forward torpedo compartment ready.

'Very good. Flood up. Stand by.'

Neitzel would come back to take up his action station and Loeffler would be more concerned with that starboard engine than his other duties in the control room, technical and complicated though they were. Ehrenberger turned the periscope following his commander's orders. And Wolz, the skipper, looked again at the dramatically high-lighted bulks of the convoy from the last flames dying away of a sinking ship.

Once more he must thrust himself into the inferno.

His calculations were beginning to obsess him and he found, as U-55 ran in on a converging course, that he did not much care for that, not at all.

With the addition of the ammunition ship, a five thousand tonner, and the freighter, which he could

45

only assess at four thousand at most, his total now stood at twenty-one thousand two hundred.

Nearly half-way there to the first magic figure.

Once again he attacked from downmoon with the labouring ships silhouetted against the shifting light.

'Steer one-seven-five.'

'Steer one-seven-five.'

Ghostlike, sinister, U-55 slid through the swell towards the port side of the convoy.

The shape of the convoy had been lost. Ships struggled along, not caring where they were so long as they kept away from the horrendous effects of the U-boats. Some huddled; some broke away and steamed on their own courses and their own best speeds. The convoy was breaking apart.

Baldur Wolz had studied very carefully everything he could lay his hands on and everything he could listen to that would teach him how to handle a U-boat. His father had been run down by a criminally careless German vessel just at the tail end of the last war. That was why Wolz had been brought up by his aunt and uncle. He had read Admiral Bauer's book *Das Unterseeboot* published in Berlin in 1931. He had listened from an early age to stories told by old friends of his father, men who had taken their first world war U-boats in to the attack. He had read Donitz. From the tactics developed in 1918 of night attack on the surface, the profits and the harvest were being reaped right now, at this very minute, as the ocean filled with burning and sinking British ships.

But there was more to it, even, than that.

That fat tanker he had seen as he'd turned away from the convoy . . .

The centre columns were far more intact than the flanks, as was to be expected. The A.M.C. still steamed on. The admiral in command would have his ship in there, at the van. The valuable ships were in the centre.

Baldur Wolz ran in boldly past a disintegrating escort screen, passed under the counter of a Norwegian vessel,

46

and struck for the centre of the convoy.

'Steer one-oh-oh.'

'Steer one-oh-oh.'

Now U-55 purred along parallel with the columns. The dark bulks of ships rose to either hand. At the distance apart of the columns, something like a thousand metres, detection of the surfaced U-boat boldly sailing along midway between, in company, was still surprisingly difficult. By maintaining equal speed, Wolz kept the betraying wash right down. He searched for the tanker.

There!

She boiled along, smoke pouring from her squat funnel situated right aft. Her bridge structure towered from the centre of her long deck. A ten thousand tonner if she was anything. Wolz lowered his glasses and bent to the pipe.

'Tanker, on starboard bow. Do you have her?'

'Got her, skipper. What a beauty for an eel!'

'I shall be turning just forrard of her. Mind you don't miss, Kern. We shall have to make a very smart course reversal – keep on your toes, Obersteuermann.'

'Very good, Herr Oberleutnant!'

Once again before he committed his last torpedoes, apart from the eel in the stern tube, Wolz studied the tactical situation through his night glasses.

No one in any of the British ships noticed him.

A lean dark shadow, he slid smoothly along, like a wolf among sheep.

The tall bulk of the A.M.C. rose from the water. Lightless, hulking, her funnel outlined bleakly against the moon-hazed sky, she bore on. Her guns would prove unpleasant if sharp eyes on her bridge spotted him. But Wolz was gaining confidence with every passing moment. It seemed that the English lookouts must be asleep, or dreaming. Certainly, they did not give any indication they had a U-boat less than a quarter of a mile from them.

Maybe the low shape of the U-boat was impossible to spot. He was trimmed down. The conning tower was

47

a small dark object in the sea. The English ships towered up like blocks of sailing skyscrapers, tall, vulnerable, ready for destruction.

'Beginning attack,' he said. His voice remained calm. 'Bring her around easily.'

'On, on, on,' called Ehrenberger.

The sights came on . . .

'Loose!'

'Steer two-eight-oh.'

'Steer two-eight-oh.'

U-55 surged around. A vagrant wave broke against the conning tower. Wolz held his breath.

Now the boat was running back through the convoy.

The seconds ticked away.

With eye-searing brilliance the tanker erupted.

The fish had caught her just abaft the bridge.

She burst into flames and smoke, a massive eruption of fire that boiled to the heavens. Everything lay exposed under that merciless glare.

Even as the second concussion followed, puny after the blaze of the tanker, yet just as deadly, the port after lookout screamed: 'Got her! The cruiser! Got her!'

The starboard forward lookout yelled: 'Destroyer! Starboard bow!'

Wolz jerked about. His eyes ran with the coruscating images of the tanker's death.

For a few vital moments he could not see.

His mind grappled with the calculations, the lines of the convoy, the position of U-55, the position of the oncoming destroyer.

It seemed impossible to him she would fail to spot him now. The light from the burning tanker would be to his stern, and he would be silhouetted against that deadly glow.

He opened his mouth to yell: 'Flood! Dive!'

And then he paused.

He could see.

The destroyer was one of the small whaling type vessels the Royal Navy had flung desperately into the

48

battle as escorts. Confident again, he gave fresh helm orders, swung U-55 away.

'Give me your best speed, Kurt! Come on, Chief! Give me everything you've got!'

On the surface, impudently, outracing the starshell, U-55 sailed away from the struggling corvette.

At a cracking eighteen knots U-55 poured on the speed and roared away from *Nemesia's* paltry fourteen knots.

On *Nemesia's* tiny bucking bridge Lieutenant-Commander Dunton peered desperately into the luridly inflamed darkness.

The damned U-boat had to be on this side of the convoy. The track angles of the torpedoes that had kippered the tanker and *Archon* indicated that. Yet he could see no sign of her.

Abruptly, the port lookout bellowed.

'Submarine! Red two-oh!'

Every eye on the bridge switched across.

Yes! There it was, the tiny black hump that could only be a U-boat's conning tower!

'There's the bastard! Guns! Open fire.'

At the order the crew of the forward – and only – four inch gun leaped into action. The ranges and bearing were called off. The layers spun their wheels. The loading number slammed the shell in. He was a seaman who, a few months ago, had been sweeping the floors of a tea warehouse in London, sampling his firm's wares as often as possible, looking forward to Saturday night at the pictures. He was eager, anxious to do well. He slammed the shell in hurriedly and the breech clanged on its shutting arc before the brass cartridge case was fully seated home in the breech.

The shell jammed.

'Come on! Come on you dozy lot of half-awake idiots!' screamed the Sub-lieutenant who was Gunnery Officer in H.M.S. *Nemesia*. A few months ago he had been sitting at his desk in an insurance company's glass-walled offices in Leadenhall Street. Now he raved

4   49

and threatened and pleaded; but the breech remained jammed.

'What's wrong?' shouted Dunton. These chaps were all thumbs. And yet he would still prefer to be here, on the bridge of *Nemesia*, than the bridge of the old East Indies rustbucket he had so recently left.

The uproar on deck continued. *Nemesia* swung about astern of the U-boat. The conning tower frothed a wash of white in the darkness. The Jerry was running away from them.

'Get that breech cleared!' shrieked the Gunnery Officer.

Nemesia trembled and shook and shivered as her single reciprocating engine laboured to deliver more than the designed 2,750 I.H.P.

Dunton leaned over the bridge.

The Gunnery Officer's face would have sent all the typists in the insurance company's typing pool screaming in panic. They would never have recognised him. But, for all that, the gun remained jammed, and the bastard of a U-boat drew steadily ahead, pulling away past the flames and the enormous wind-blowing racket of burning from the doomed tanker.

Dunton turned back to his Number One. He had regained control of himself.

'Sometimes, Number One,' he said in a voice that did not deceive his second in command, 'sometimes I regret they abandoned flogging in the Royal Navy.'

'Quite, sir,' said Number One, and then found something extremely urgent to do elsewhere.

Nothing sounded on asdic. The pings rang with that empty, hollow note of mockery they always held when no echo came bouncing back.

Lieutenant-Commander Dunton gave a new course to the quartermaster, a course that would take them back to the convoy. 'Come down to ten knots,' he said. He felt the injustice of it all. He was prepared to blow his engine and boilers to kingdom come to catch a U-boat; but the cheeky bastards just ran away from him.

And he was realist enough to know that his single little four-incher would have made no difference at all even if it had fired, except for the divine providence of a lucky shot.

This ship's company needed a very great deal more work and drilling and training before they could meet even half-way the menace of the U-boats.

Dunton knew with an uncomfortable feeling of fate blowing down his neck, that they would get plenty of practice in the weeks and months ahead.

If they weren't kippered first, that was.

'That, skipper,' said Ehrenberger with a deep and glowing satisfaction, 'makes it a good forty-five thousand.'

'Maybe you rate the A.M.C. too highly.' Wolz felt the elation bubbling in him. 'You are prepared to go to fourteen thousand? I judged her one of the Cunard vessels. *Aurania*, possibly. If she was some other vessel,' here Wolz's fingers flicked pages, the silhouettes flickering over like fish leaping a millpool, 'say *Antenor*, that would give us only 11,174 tons.'

'Fourteen, skipper,' said Ehrenberger, confidently. 'And she went down, too – after she went up.'

Wolz thought about his last remaining eel, nestling in the lone stern tube.

They had done well, no doubt of that. To notch up forty-five – say forty to be on the safe side, when all the accounts were in – on a first patrol, was really a great achievement. Of course, the escorts had only themselves to blame; themselves or those in power in the British Admiralty who sent men to sea to catch U-boats in ships which were slower than the boats they were supposed to hunt.

Had U-55 been forced to dive, the story might have ended differently.

But Wolz was now convinced that he had the beating of the escorts on the surface. He did not relish the idea of facing depth charge attacks – he had already gone through some hair-raising experiences – but such was his confidence he was prepared to take a heavy bet they'd come through that safely.

'After all, Kern,' he said, letting his thoughts spill over into words, knowing his Number One would follow him. 'She failed to open fire on us. I don't understand that.'

'Maybe the gunlayer caught his finger in the breech?'

'The British Navy? Hardly.'

'Well, then, some other portion of his anatomy. Whatever the reason, she didn't open fire and we got clean away.'

The night had been one of hard work and tension for the crew of U-55. For the seamen in the convoy the night had been one of horror and terror and death.

Baldur Wolz did not think of that. He had a job to do and however distasteful sinking fine ships might be, it was a job that had to be done and a task set to his hands.

He would do it.

He would do that dreadful work to the utmost of his ability.

CHAPTER SIX

In the morning, the routine signals over 4995kc/s brought fresh instructions to Wolz. He had made his own report with a smug feeling of satisfaction.

Now he called sharply to Ehrenberger.

'Seems we still have a job to do out here, Kern, even with only one eel left.'

'Yes, skipper?'

'We are to remain on station to signal weather reports.

We're to become a mobile weather station.'

Ehrenberger made a face.

'Maybe we should have shot off that last eel into the thick of them, skipper.'

Wolz shook his head. This was a decision he had made.

'No. I'm not loosing off until I've a ship in my sights. And the bigger the better. With all the fuss going on there was no certainty we'd have hit anything by browning them.'

Ehrenberger nodded. He was getting to know this devilish-looking young skipper of his better all the time.

'You're right, of course. What course, skipper?'

'Steer two-seven-five until the watch changes. Then we'll turn south. If the weather is coming in from the west all day then BdU will want to know the first sign of a change.'

'Very good.'

The excitement of the night had drained many of the men. They had tasted victory, and the taste was sweet and heady. Strictly in turn, one man at a time, they were allowed up on to the bridge for a smoke and a few lungfuls of fresh air.

Whilst they did that the Officer of the Watch made very sure they kept their eyes open. There could be no idle hands or eyes in a U-boat.

When he had his thoughts in order, Wolz spoke to the men over the loud-hailer system. In each compartment the men automatically looked up, grimed, bearded, sweaty; but certain and sure, confident in their own strengths.

'We have struck a great blow for the Fatherland. According to preliminary estimates we have achieved a total of forty to forty-five thousand tons.'

He could imagine the smiles, the back-slapping, the joyful shouts of triumph.

He went on doggedly.

'But this is only a beginning. We shall be returning in due time to Lorient. Until that time we have vitally important work to do out here.'

Now some of the smiles would tremble, perhaps vanish. Everyone had been looking forward to a quick return to base. The delights of Occupied France had only been sampled as yet.

'We must stay on station and transmit weather reports. These are absolutely vital for the conduct of the U-boat offensive. And, I promise you, the moment an opportunity offers to sink our last eel into the fat guts of an Englishman, we shall take that opportunity. I thank you for your loyal support during the conflict. That is all.'

Strictly speaking, the penultimate sentence had been totally unnecessary. If they hadn't done their work properly then they'd be facing the wrath of Oberleutnant Baldur Wolz right now.

And they knew it.

Every last one of them.

Leutnant Kurt Loeffler came forward to report.

His face told Wolz the bad news.

'That spurt last night, skipper. I've been working on the crankshaft; but the split is there and won't go away. It's in a devilish difficult – well, you saw it for yourself.'

Wolz nodded.

There was no chance of strengthening the shaft there.

'So we're down to one diesel?'

' 'Fraid so, skipper.'

'We've spent a great deal of time on the surface, so the batteries should be in good heart. But, Kurt, make sure they're absolutely topped up. If we have to dive and go deep and hang around waiting for some infernal English destroyer to shove off, we may not get a good opportunity to recharge for some time.'

'That's understood.'

'Good. Make it so.'

Not for the first or last time, Wolz reflected that the Chief was a good fellow. He had brought U-55 safely back from Narvik after they'd so unsuccessfully made the attempt to torpedo H.M.S. *Warspite*. Their reception back in Kiel had been enthusiastic – but in a limited and contained way. The enormous events going on on the battlefields of Belgium and France had occupied everyone's attention. Donitz, at least, had been pleased a U-boat he had just about written off had been saved. There was talk of a decoration. He gained the impression that his chances of commanding his own boat had been brought measurably nearer.

So he had been sent off on leave, expecting to be called back at any moment, willing to be called back.

The over-running of the French Army, the chase of the remnants of the British Army, the evacuation at Dunkirk, these were the events that filled people's minds.

He had found his uncle's schloss deserted by all serving officers. It struck him as strange that he, a representative of the German Armed Forces who had so far been the only ones in action after the Polish campaign, should now be the only one idle when these huge events filled the world's stage.

This leave, unlike the last, he had gone off to Castle Hartstein to see Trudi at once.

She was not at home.

The old dodderer Heinrich mumbled away as usual in the vast, gloomy hall with the staircase where he had said such outrageous things to Trudi von Hartstein. Karin, the maidservant, nursemaid, housekeeper, the overseer of everything that went on in the castle, came in. This time her wizened nutcracker face was not so set against this young man.

A sprig of the Herrenvolk, she had called him.

'Fraulein Hartstein?'

'She has gone away with her mother, the baroness. I am not at liberty to tell you, Mein Herr.'

'But – '

'She told me to say that she was well. But it is impossible for her to contact you. That was what she said.'

To Wolz's surprise, Karin did not, as he would have expected, take great joy from, in effect, telling him to push off.

He had left, instructing Karin to make sure that

Fraulein Trudi knew he had called, and had sent her his very best regards.

His very best regards!

Did he mean that?

He had thought that the instant he saw Trudi again, with her pale face and golden hair and intoxicating figure, he would immediately ask her to marry him. That would depress Lottie for a morning, perhaps for part of the afternoon as well. But Lottie would understand. And then, on his stupid stubborn way to see Trudi at last, he had stumbled across the black Mercedes, and the machine-pistol fire, and seen Trudi's three friends killed – machine-gunned and burned to death.

The local doctor, an old friend of the family, Doctor Engel, had cautioned him that nothing must be said. The Fraulein Trudi had fallen from a horse and cut her head. That was the story.

There was danger, real and horrible, if the truth got out.

The burned car, the three dead bodies, all had been spirited away.

Who had done all these things, Wolz did not know.

Driving back to his uncle's schloss, he reflected that perhaps he would never know. He had no way of getting into contact with Trudi. If she wished to see him again then it was all down to her.

He sensed in a way that made him angry that perhaps it was the very foundations of the glorious Third Reich, in which he passionately believed, that allowed such things to happen.

Certainly, he had known one or two, not many, cadets at academy who had hinted at the surface of the new Germany being a very different picture from the deeper and darker depths.

He shrugged that off.

There was always crime, although that had gone down with the new Party methods. And the war demanded everything a man could give.

This leave was not turning out at all as he had expected.

With the arrival of Cousin Siegfried, snatching a few days leave, and bringing with him not only Marlene but four of her friends with her, the schloss once more erupted into its usual hectic activity.

Cousin Manfred was very busy with his Messerschmitt Bf 109 flying with the Luftwaffe. Cousin Helmut, as usual, was doing things of which he did not speak somewhere or other. From a few chance words, Wolz gathered he was in France.

So the regular hangers on, the cronies, the invited guests, who always turned up when Siegfried was at home, had the place to themselves. The fat infantry major had left. Now the schloss was almost all SS or Party officials and their wives and girl friends.

Wolz expected that Marlene, who was undeniably beautiful as to body, and more and more ravaged in her features, would go through her dance and song routine again. She had patched things up with her manager, and was back on the stage again. How much she drank, how many cigarettes she smoked, what else she got up to, Wolz told himself was no concern of his.

He had told Siegfried that Marlene had been very down and had talked wildly of suicide.

Siegfried, in his heavy way, had nodded and said that he would deal with the situation.

He must have done something. Marlene had never looked so ravishing.

'Aren't you pleased to see me, Baldur?' she greeted him. She wore a dress that enhanced what nature had endowed her with, her hair shining and curled, blonde, scented. 'I hear you did something spectacular. There might be a medal in it – the Ritterkreuz, perhaps?'

'Hardly, Marlene. Second Class, if I'm lucky, along with everyone else. Yes, I'm glad to see you looking so well.'

'Oh!' She narrowed her eyes at him.

He tried to phrase it compassionately.

'I thought our last talk . . . no more like that? Not now?'

She shook her head.

'I'm not going to jump off a cliff or throw myself under a car, Baldur. I've decided. Siegfried has been very good to me – he doesn't love me, you know. There's someone else. He won't tell me. Well, you'd hardly expect him to, would you? But I know.'

So did Wolz. Siegfried had a very real interest in Trudi von Hartstein. What Cousin Siegfried didn't know about Trudi would fill a U-boat training manual and, no doubt, all Manfred's Luftwaffe manuals as well.

'I don't bear him a grudge. But it makes life a little uncertain.'

'Siegfried will always – '

'Oh, yes.' Marlene chucked her half-smoked cigarette away and immediately started fishing in her bag for her case. 'He'll always take care of me. I tell myself that. But there's no guarantee in this life.'

'I suppose not. But Siegfried – '

She snapped the case. It was platinum. 'Don't let's talk of Siegfried just now. We'll put on our show for his friends. He's earned quite a name for himself. Did you know he'll be made up to SS Obersturmbannfuhrer soon?'

Wolz didn't know; but it did not surprise him. Cousin Siegfried was on his way up in the SS. SS Obersturmbann-fuhrer was equivalent to Lieutenant-Colonel. Very high-powered indeed.

Marlene moved towards the door. She began to undo the buttons on that new and fetching dress. Wolz reached the door first.

'Oh, don't be silly, Baldur! Not here, like this! I must change, that's all . . . I'll let you out.' She pulled an arm free and took the cigarette from her lips, began to wriggle the other arm out. What she had to offer had been seen many times by Siegfried and his friends – and on occasion by Wolz. 'Just remember, Baldur, any time you want me, I'll be around. And I don't say that to everyone. You know that.'

He managed to say: 'I'll remember that, Marlene,'

and walk away with a smile for her.

Going down the stairs and to the immense room where the noise of the gathering met him like surf on a rocky beach, Wolz wondered – and with sharp and pleasurably critical anticipation – what Marlene's four friends would be like.

'Steer one-eight-oh.'

'Steer one-eight-oh.'

U-55 nosed on to her new course, due south. Baldur Wolz, in his corner of the bridge, looked upon the sea and the sky and felt a remarkably detached contentment. Poor Marlene. What Siegfried had said to her to bring her out of the depths of depression she'd been wallowing in when Wolz had last seen her, he could not know. Neither had told him.

Whatever it was, it had worked.

'Permission to come on to the bridge!' bellowed up the voice of Loeffler from the conning tower.

Wolz looked about. He fixed his eye on the young Fahnrich, Otto von Magdorf. The midshipman had a skin like a girl's, clear blue eyes, a decided view of life, which indicated that he was destined for eventual command as Grand Admiral of the German Navy, and needed to have a lot of nonsense knocked out of him and a deal more of the spirit of the U-boat arm knocked into him. Wolz just hoped he was not another Adolf Forstner.

'Below with you, mid,' he said. 'Come on up, Chief.'

Von Magdorf favoured his commander with a decidedly fishy eye and went below. Out here there was no chance of an English aeroplane heaving up suddenly – the old Sunderland would be in dire trouble out here – but Wolz intended to keep to discipline and his ideas of active service. Perhaps, if they ventured someway more to the west, he might consider having a make and mend on the casing. But the very idea sent a shudder through his U-boat man's bones.

'Well, Chief, and what disaster is it this time?'

Wolz eyed Loeffler.

'Or,' he added with a tone in his voice that indicated he was not altogether in a playful mood. 'Is this merely an example of throwing your rank about? The fresh air is very good today.'

'It is very good every day for we poor chaps stuck down inside.'

'True.'

'No sympathy is to be expected.' Loeffler hurried along then as Wolz began to change his expression, as the noxious black cigar took an abrupt upward slant. 'It's number three pump, skipper. Never been right just out of dockyard hands. The valve-fitting you went ashore specially for may be the trouble. Workmanship these days is not what it was.'

'The valve-fitting may have been used in ways not intended,' said Wolz, cryptically.

'Oh?' Loeffler looked interested, as though about to enter a highly technical discussion.

'Yes, Chief. But I'm sure you don't want to know.'

'No, skipper.' Loeffler hesitated.

'Don't tell me there's more?'

The Chief abruptly took on a conspiratorial air. His gingery hair and beard, his red face, glowed. Always liable to copious sweating, his broad face broke into a sheen of perspiration, tiny drops glittering in the beard.

'I'd like a word in private with you, skipper. When it suits you.'

'You're very mysterious.'

'Nothing serious yet. But – '

Wolz took a good long look around the horizon, doing a thorough job, aware that the lookouts stiffened up as his intolerant gaze swept across their sectors. He let the Chief wait.

Then: 'Very good. I'll come down. Midshipman von Magdorf. On the bridge at the double.'

The commander and the engineer slid rapidly down the ladder through the conning tower and into the control room. When their feet hit the steel plating the

60

midshipman gripped the rungs and hauled himself up.

Wolz led the way to the wardroom, went into the tiny cramped cubby he called his cabin and when Loeffler squeezed in, drew the green curtain. If they kept their voices down, the hum of machinery should give them enough privacy.

'Now, Chief, spit it out.'

'Yes, skipper.'

And Loeffler was struck dumb, and gazed vacantly around the space where every single thing that existed there was known to him, as a drawing on a blueprint and as a steel artefact in his capable hands. Everything, that is, with the exception of the commander's personal possessions. And they were few . . .

'Come on, Kurt. I won't bite your head off.'

'I'm rather afraid you might. It's Neitzel.'

At once the levity left Wolz. He eyed his engineering officer keenly.

'Serious?'

'I don't know. It could be, I think.' Loeffler took a breath. 'Yes. I wouldn't have raised it otherwise.'

'I didn't think so. Well?'

The oddest feeling of impending doom hit Wolz. The Third Officer had promised to be a problem. With Ehrenberger, the First, with Riepold, the Second, with Loeffler, the Chief, Wolz felt he knew where he stood. They were men dedicated as he was. But Neitzel had, from the very first, not fitted in. And it was precisely because he knew how he felt about the Third Officer that Wolz had made himself, viciously, wait and see.

Loeffler's face was scarlet. He sweated.

'This is a terrible thing, skipper, for one officer to – to betray another. The honour is – '

'If someone is going to foul up my boat, I want to know!'

'Yes. That's the only reason – '

'I know!'

Then, deciding he had best help the Chief out as best he could, Wolz said firmly: 'Is it that business of the

61

torpedo running wild and killing poor Gerhardt?'

'I think that maybe tipped him over.'

'Like that, is it? I can't say I've noticed.'

'You were on the bridge. During the action I had occasion to notice the Herr Leutnant. I think – and this is only my opinion, but I hold it strongly – I think in the next attack he'll crack wide open.'

Wolz looked down.

Thank God, he thought with some savagery, thank God for someone as sensitive and sensible as Loeffler. Anyone whose honour was so finicky they would not report the incipient breakdown of a fellow officer had no place in a U-boat.

'You've spoken to Kern? To Ludwig?'

Again Loeffler hesitated.

'No, skipper. I think Kern had a suspicious eye on Neitzel; but then, you chaps were all so busy . . .'

'Yes, it was a slap-up affair. Forty thousand tons, at least.'

That was mere verbiage to cover his thoughts.

He made up his mind.

'First of all, Kurt, I want to thank you for coming to me like this. I know it wasn't easy. As for the Herr Leutnant, he is behaving perfectly normally now. That is to be expected. But now we've been alerted we can keep an eye on him next time. Anyway, we're hardly likely to find anything out here that will cause any problems.'

'That is true.'

'And we both know any man is likely to crack at any time. Once the depth charges start rolling down . . . Well, no one likes to think of that.'

'Gott strafe England, eh?'

'Right. If the balloon goes up on this cruise again we'll keep a very sharp eye out. I'll have a word with him at some stage – very casual.'

'I understand.'

'You can't always tell. A man can be on the edge for

attack after attack, and another will snap right away. It takes all sorts.'

When Loeffler had gone, Wolz sat for a few moments, staring unseeingly at his desk.

The desk was that by courtesy only, being a folding table; but on it had been written many letters to Lisl and Trudi and his cousins. The log was written up there. What was he going to write in the log about this situation?

Nothing at the moment. Of course. But, if he had to, he would put it all in. Donitz had no time for half-hearted U-boat commanders.

All the weather data they could collect was duly despatched over the radio to U-boat Headquarters. Encouraging signals were taken in, and Wolz exerted himself to convince the crew that the work they were doing was a valuable part of the total war effort.

They turned on to a reciprocal course of due north and then counter-marched again, running on the port engine. The water supply eased off. Wolz kept an eye on Neitzel in the most friendly of fashions.

It was perfectly possible that the fellow would be quite all right the next time. Wolz did not for a moment believe the Chief had been mistaken. He hedged around the question with Ehrenberger, and Number One contented himself with a non-committal answer that tempted Wolz to the belief that Ehrenberger, too, had a weather eye open in the same quarter.

Four days later BdU signalled that U-55 should return to Lorient. Any targets were to be attacked en route.

'I'm not going back with an eel stuffed away uselessly in the stern tube, Number One!' declared Wolz.

He realised now that he should have loosed the torpedo when he had the chance. It might have hit something during that last wild escapade. And, of course, there was the ever present problem that the thing would malfunction.

The depth-setting mechanism often failed, so that

the eel ran too deep, and with the contact pistols fitted that was useless. Even a magnetic type, in working order, couldn't fire the charge if the fish was too deep in the water.

Wolz had suffered the remarkable experience of being chased by one of his own torpedoes that had circled one hundred and eighty degrees and gone bald-headed for him. Now, if only the scientists of the Kriegsmarine could come up with a torpedo that did that to order! He'd enjoy setting one of those off circling in a convoy. The eel would be bound to hit something then!

The course was laid off and everyone was fully alive to the luxury of not having to negotiate the dangerous waters of the Rose Garden, north about Scotland, to gain their base. Now they could chug gently across Biscay and reach their brand new bases on the west coast of France. That was what the Panzers had done for the Navy, and Wolz, for one, was pleased to hand them their due credit.

Kapitanleutnant Lemp had been the first U-boat commander to enter a French Naval base, bringing his U-30 in at the end of June. Lemp, with U-30, had also been the first to strike in the war, sinking *Athenia* only moments after the English had made their big mistake and declared war. There would be some grand reunions in Lorient. Many U-boat commanders were building up big scores, and Prien was no longer a solitary ace. With a sudden pang he did not recognise, and made no attempt to understand, Wolz looked forward hungrily to those informal gatherings of U-boat commanders.

These men were, indeed, an élite.

'Object on the port bow!' Otto von Magdorf sang out with tremendous satisfaction at being the first man in the boat to spot a ship. 'Ship! Looks like a big freighter.'

Every eye swung to the spot. A lone ship! An independent, a runner – a ship marked for destruction!

CHAPTER SEVEN

As he took his command in towards the lone ship, Wolz kept an extraordinarily sharp watch out. So far during the course of the sea war, most tonnage sunk by U-boats had been chopped down in the form of ships sailing independently. But the British were continually extending their convoy system and the attack in which U-55 had so recently taken part was one of the very first real convoy battles.

The law of the sea had ceased to operate as far as English shipping was concerned, by order of the Führer, and U-boats were empowered to sink enemy and neutral alike, at once and without warning. Much as a seaman like Baldur Wolz might regret the necessity, the harsh realities of war made this unholy course the only one possible for U-boats. He had already, when the orders had been promulgated, made up his mind he would continue to do all he could for the survivors. But he was now under no constraints whatsoever.

Obeying his orders he could stalk up on this ship and shoot a torpedo into her and watch her sink and sail away.

That this was precisely what he had been doing in the attacks on the convoys was an entirely different matter. They appeared to him as two distinct and separate acts of war.

Even the ancient six-inch gun mounted high on the old steamer's fantail could not alter that feeling.

'What do you make of her, Number One?'

Ehrenberger squinted through the glasses.

'She oughtn't to be out here alone without a nurse-maid.'

Wolz laughed.

65

'I'd say she's a grandmother herself and needs the protection of a nursing sister. She's mighty long in the tooth.'

That, of course, made no difference. She was carrying war materials to England and therefore must be sunk.

'No smoke, skipper – and she doesn't appear to be under way.'

Wolz looked.

'Right. She's hove to.'

'And look at that list.'

Wolz reached the obvious conclusion.

'She's no independent. She hasn't the speed for one thing. She's been hit in convoy and abandoned.'

Ehrenberger lowered his glasses.

'I'd like to see the faces of the crew if they could see her now. They must have had their pants alight when they abandoned ship.'

'On this track – h'mm – ' Wolz considered as U-55 purred over the sunlit sea. 'Yes. I think she must be from the convoy we hit. The position is about right.'

Ehrenberger prepared to descend the tower to his battle station. He cocked an interrogative eye at his commander, and spoke in a low voice.

'Are you going to let Leutnant Neitzel handle the eel, skipper?'

Wolz kept his face immobile. So Ehrenberger was aware . . .

'Gun action, Kern! Two reasons: one, the eel might not behave, and, two, we'll save her and hope she does behave when we have a real target. Yes?'

'Very good!'

Wolz gave the quartermaster a course to steer that would bring U-55 up fine on the starboard bow. There they would be outside the arc of fire of the stern gun. Not that he anticipated much accuracy from the scratch crew manning the ancient six-incher; but a single brick from the gun could do untold harm to the U-boat. At the very least, it would be uncomfortable, and if they were prevented from diving, returning to base would become highly dangerous, far more problematical than usual.

At action stations the steel shark ghosted in towards her prey.

Steadying the glasses, Wolz focussed on the rust-streaked bow plates.

'*Belphegor.*'

The book was checked.

'Built in Marseilles before we were born, skipper. Four thousand one hundred tons.'

The calculations were made almost before the words were out.

'Not quite,' said Wolz.

'But nearly – and with the last eel –'

'Quite.'

'And she's French.'

'Well,' said Wolz, reflectively. 'She was sailing in an English convoy from America. I'd say that makes her a hostile, quite apart from the orders about neutrals. We'll sink her.' He leaned over the bridge coaming to shout down to the Number One who had taken up his gun action station by the 8.8 centimetre. 'Stitch a few holes along her waterline. Make her look like a postage stamp.'

'Very good!'

No sign of life appeared in the ship. Her crew had taken to the boats all right, the davits were empty. She rolled uneasily in the swell. At fifteen hundred metres Ehrenberger opened fire.

The spiteful crack of the 8.8 centimetre gun shattered across the calm water.

A waterspout rose alongside the rusted black plating of *Belphegor*.

'Again, Kern! Hit her!'

The gun roared again and the stink of burnt powder drifted flatly, acrid in nostril and eye.

Wolz swung about abruptly.

Midshipman Otto von Magdorf was staring with a tense, white-faced expression at the ship.

'This is not your sector, mid!' bellowed Wolz. 'Keep your eyes skinned where they belong. I shall not warn you a second time.'

'Yes, Herr Oberleutnant.'

Von Magdorf swung back to the port side, his face scarlet. Wolz saw the way his fists gripped the Zeiss, knuckles like tallow, and he promised he'd sort the little prig out very quickly indeed if he gave any trouble.

The gunner had the range nicely now and was pumping the shells into the French ship's waterline. A long running swell lifted U-55 unexpectedly as the gun belched flame and smoke.

The shell smacked into the upperworks abaft the bridge, splinters and smoke flew gouting into the air.

Wolz made no comment. That could happen to anybody and the gunner, Joachim Henschel, was a good shot and a disciplinary correction now would be less than useful. The gun rapped out again; the shell blew in another section of the waterline plating.

Ehrenberger was yelling.

Wolz checked.

Then he bellowed: 'Cease fire!'

A white figure appeared on the rail of the ship, leaning over, waving.

Even as he stared through the Zeiss, Wolz felt the sick feeling of helplessness grip him.

A woman!

There could be no mistake. She wore some kind of jacket over what looked to be a long white dress. Then, shocked, he realised what she was wearing.

A nightdress!

What had been going on in *Belphegor*?

'That's a woman!' bellowed Ehrenberger. The cry was taken up by the gun's crew.

For a moment everyone on the bridge and around the gun was stricken with the marvel of it.

'Silence!' rapped Wolz.

The ship was listing further. Already well over, she

68

would be gone very soon. There would be no need to fire again.

If the U-boat arm of the Kriegsmarine was a swearing service, Baldur Wolz would be cursing and foaming right now.

What a thing to happen!

Right out here in the Atlantic – a woman!

And, if his guess was right, a Frenchwoman.

They had been looking forward to making the acquaintance of some French girls in Lorient. Wolz had no wish in the whole wide world to meet one here.

He couldn't just sink the ship and leave her, could he?

Was there a U-boat commander in these circumstances who could do that?

Water lapped well up the waterline of the French ship. The decks showed clearly in all their confusion of abandoned raffle. No time to have the airboat broken out and pumped up. He bent to the voicepipe.

'Quartermaster, steer alongside! And steer small! Chief, get ready for a little fancy diesel working. I shall group in the motors if I have to.'

With swift, precise steering instructions to the helmsman, Obersteuermann Willi Wilshaus, Wolz brought U-55 to lie alongside the ship. She was no more than a drifting hulk now. He gained some relief in her lee. The two vessels, one large, ponderous, and toppling ever further and further to destruction, and the other, lean, trim, wolfish, sailed in a gruesome company together.

'Secure from the gun! Get ready to receive a passenger!'

Wolz glared aloft. Despite the list, the girl was still too high to jump, and he wondered if she would have the strength to shin down any of the dangling falls.

'Mademoiselle!' he bellowed up, furious, angry, filled with the desire to get his boat away from this ludicrously dangerous spot. 'You must climb down! The ship is sinking. You must hurry!'

His French could withstand that kind of demand; if she started jabbering nineteen to the dozen he'd be sunk.

The ship rolled. She loomed above the U-boat. For a horrified instant Wolz thought the whole lot would roll right over on top of him. Then, groaning in her injured, abused and battered ribs and scantlings, she righted herself. Water spumed and foamed between the two vessels.

'Jump! Grab a line and jump!'

The girl waved. Then, thankfully, she understood what was required of the situation. She ran along the deck and climbed the rail, reaching for a thick and greasy rope dangling from the line between the davits.

Heinrich Tauch from the guncrew grabbed the end of the line as it snaked. Wolz frowned. That was quick thinking; but it made the climb down more difficult.

The girl tucked her nightdress about her waist. Long legs gleamed in the pale sunshine. Then she was half-climbing, half-sliding down the rope. Twice Wolz thought she had lost her grip and was gone, and twice she recovered, to pause for a few heartbeats before resuming. He saw she had climbed down ropes before. A tomboy, then?

No other more sinister explanation entered his mind.

When, at last, she was near enough to be swayed in with only a last minute soaking to drench her, Wolz was glad he had not ordered one of his men up the rope to fetch her. He cared for her safety; he cared for the welfare of his crew far more.

She landed all in a heap by the gun and Ehrenberger lifted her up. He held her correctly, around the waist, and her short dark hair plastered across her scalp glittered. She stood up. She was shaking. That was to be expected. The thin nightdress was, like her hair, plastered to her.

The shape revealed sent a hot thump through Wolz.

The narrowness of her waist, the length of her legs, the full upward tilting breasts, made him realise he had brought a tremendous problem into his boat.

As to himself, he fancied he could control whatever desires might be aroused. And his crew? Of course, they

70

were honest sailormen, products of the Kriegsmarine training schools and academies. The girl would receive the correct attention in U-55.

All the same, the quicker she was given more seemly clothing the better.

Immediately the girl was safe Wolz conned his boat away from the sinking vessel.

'Clear the gun!' he bellowed down. 'Herr Leutnant Riepold. Take the girl to my cabin. Find her some clothes. And then stand guard outside.'

'Very good.'

Riepold hustled the girl below. As she passed Wolz he saw her face, oval, dusky, with the black hair like wet paint over her head. Her deep brown eyes regarded him hesitantly, her lips half-parted and the tip of a tongue showing.

'Thank you, m'sieu – ' she began.

'Below with you, mademoiselle. I will speak to you later.'

Riepold assisted her down the ladder, perfectly properly.

Wolz dragged his mind away from the shape of her – my God, what a beauty!

Belphegor was going.

Ehrenberger said, thoughtfully, obviously saying one thing and thinking of another. 'I think she's a ship we had a crack at, skipper. The torpedo must have malfunctioned and the crew thought they were done for.'

'Yes,' agreed Wolz, 'during the attack when the munitions ship went up. That was enough to make them think they'd been hit.'

The old ship listed further and further. Her upperworks lay on the sea with all their age and tiredness at last finding rest. She turned over and sank without trouble, like a very old person dying peacefully in bed. Her fires were out and she was not in steam so there was no explosion as she settled. A widening disturbance in the water, a circle of expanding ripples, and she was gone.

Wolz turned away.

The sight of a ship sinking always affected him profoundly. Gott strafe the war, that was more like it. If only there did not have to be wars! If only the stupid democracies had listened when the Führer spoke! If only stubborn England would take the sensible course and accept a just peace now they had lost the war!

'Take the conn, Kern,' he said to Ehrenberger. 'Keep your eyes skinned. Course for Lorient.' He gave the course in its more correct form; but he'd said that with purpose. He wanted these men to understand that although they might still be at sea and fighting, they were on their way home.

Well, not home exactly, but as near as they were likely to get to home for some time, if the stupid Englishmen insisted on fighting on.

Then he went below to find out how a beautiful French girl came to be in a sinking ship in mid Atlantic in her nightgown.

CHAPTER EIGHT

The men of U-55 reacted in their various different ways as Leutnant Ludwig Riepold conducted the rescued French girl to the skipper's quarters.

Hans Lindner, seeing the girl's body exposed through the thin, soaked nightdress, compared her with his new bride and owned she was very nice, very nice.

Loeffler, making very sure he was around to see all there was to see, reflected that if they made them like that in France, and he was his usual self, then the shore time in Lorient should prove highly diverting.

Sanitatsobermaat Reche flew into the control, heading

for the wardroom. He felt it was his duty to be on hand. The mademoiselle must be in urgent need of his expert services, assuredly. After an ordeal like that, chilled to the bone with sea water, she would need a brisk rub down with alcohol and then soft ointments. Yes, Reche decided, they'd never included a situation like this in the brief course he'd taken; but he knew how to deal with it. By God, yes! He'd work the soft oils all over her body, make her feel warm again . . .

Leutnant Neitzel made very sure he got a good look at the girl. He sucked in his breath. He felt the heat bursting through him. What a beauty! The thought of holding her in his arms, of pressing her close, shook through him as a gale shakes an old tree. He had to turn away, and he wiped the sweat from his forehead and along his stubbled beard.

Otto von Magdorf looked at the girl as she went below; he had seen the long slender legs clenched around the rope, the nightdress tucked up out of the way. Now, close at hand, with the nightdress plastered to her hips and thighs, rounded sheer over her breasts, she seemed to him so marvellous a creation he had to turn away and look at the sinking ship and let the long sick tremble shake through all his limbs.

The other men in U-55 looked at the French girl in their own fashions, and laughed, and commented jovially, and went back to their work.

The old superstitions died hard at sea. Always, men had said it was unlucky to have a woman in a ship.

The general consensus of opinion of the crew of U-55 was that they could stand bad luck – for they had had their share of it along with the good – for the sake of the sight of so marvellous a creature as this in their midst.

Angelique Savinien collapsed onto the bunk pointed out to her by the fierce bearded German sailor.

She had fought back the tears. She felt cold and hot. The stink in this tiny cramped place filled with steel machinery and oily projections, and pipes – the pipes! – and the dials and gadgets and levers and the ferocious

73

white lighting, the strange stomach-churning reek of it filled her with nausea. The oddest thing was that among the stench of oil and pitch and damp there came to her sensitive nostrils the unmistakable aroma of perfume. Eau de Cologne, and lavender water; but, also, stronger, heavier perfumes, scents with which she was totally unfamiliar, not having made the acquaintance of girls who used that kind of musky allurement.

A harsh conversation in German gabbled on beyond the green curtain. She lay on the bunk and shivered.

The German reappeared. He was smiling.

He handed her a grey shirt and a pair of men's trousers – well, they would not have women's clothes aboard, would they? – and a leather jacket. He smiled and nodded and gabbled on in his harsh hateful German. She lifted her head. She reached for the rough damp towel mechanically.

She understood he wanted her to dry herself and change her clothes. That was sensible, for she'd catch cold if not pneumonia. The green curtain rustled back. Slowly, with trembling fingers, Angelique tried to pull off the damp, clinging nightdress. Her skin goose-pimpled. She shivered again.

Outside the green curtain Riepold was saying to Sanitatsobermaat Reche, with great gravity masking a giant hilarity, that, yes, he fully understood Reche's only desire was the well-being and comfort of the lady, and, yes, a rub down with alchohol and ointment might be just the thing, and no, it would be best if they waited for Daddy.

Reche tried to argue, but Riepold insisted.

Finally, Riepold told him to go away and fetch a cup of hot coffee, that being the only medicine he was prepared to allow until the skipper came down.

Angelique understood none of it.

She had seen the look in the eyes of one or two of the Germans.

She knew that look – was it not the look in the eyes of that old goat, Captain Augier?

What was to happen to her she would not, could not, think.

She had read all about what happened to those poor Belgian women at the beginning of the last war.

She was still a virgin and she had intended to remain a virgin until she married.

Maybe the decision would be taken out of her hands.

When the cabin door had jammed itself shut on her in the old *Belphegor* and she had sunk down sobbing, she had given herself up for lost.

How long she had waited there she did not know. The dawn at last came; but the blackout of her cabin persisted. She found the little torch she carried and had opened the tin of biscuits she had brought from Canada, knowing how scarce food was becoming in Europe. She had eaten and drunk a little water from the tap over the basin; but that soon ran dry.

Just when the door unjammed itself she did not know.

But she had awoken from her sleep that was more a long shocked unconsciousness to find it sliding free.

The sun on deck warmed her through. In the saloon she had gone through to the galley and found food and opened bottles of mineral water. She wandered the ship. She did not think to put any other clothes on over the jacket.

How weird! A whole ship to herself, adrift in the Atlantic!

She had slept at night, and awoken, and eaten and wandered about, and she had looked at the hostile horizons and prayed for an English ship to appear and rescue her.

Her spirits veered wildly from the deepest despair to an intoxicated belief that in the very next minute a ship would sail up, with the white Ensign fluttering, and take her off.

She had sobbed all her tears out.

She had been in the saloon, eating tinned food, when the first crashes sent shudders through the old ship.

An enormous, splintering roar had smashed at the

75

deckhouse. Shrieking in fear she had rushed out to see a cloud of smoke and flame bursting from the deckhouse abaft the bridge. More bangs hit the ship.

Over on the side that dipped so frighteningly towards the sea she gripped the rail and stared and she felt the sick dismay and the relief fighting within her.

She knew what that low, lethal grey shape was.

A submarine!

A dirty, cowardly, underhand German U-boat.

The Boche fought their war like this, sinking innocent people.

But she had waved.

For the U-boat would at least stop shooting the ship to pieces when they saw her. It would have to.

So she had been rescued.

How she had managed to cling to the greasy rope she could not remember. Many a time she had climbed up and down to her brothers' tree house at home. Now the climb down was a nightmare. But she had held on. She had hit the steel deck of the submarine and been hustled below.

She knew who the captain was by his looks, by the jut of his jaw, the look in his eyes. He looked a very devil.

Just why she had said to him thank you, she did not know.

The words had risen to her lips unbidden.

They seemed the only things she could have said at the time, Merci, monsieur – yes, odd and strange; but spoken with deep feeling.

Now she struggled out of the soaked nightdress in the miasmic inside of a horrible U-boat. The rough towel did little to dry her. She pulled the harsh grey shirt on, feeling the material rub over her nipples that were erect with the chill of it all. The trousers would only just go over her hips; but the waistband was far too wide and she hauled up the belt to the last notch and still there was an unsightly sagging around her waist which the tucked-in shirt did nothing to fill.

She trembled.

76

What would happen now?

They had given her no brassiere – there was hardly likely to be one aboard, she supposed, and they had given her no knickers. She would have to ask. Her feet were bare. Her slippers had been lost, she did not remember where.

She towelled her hair and wished she had a comb or a brush.

The man outside the green curtain kept shifting his position. Angelique did not think he was peering in at her. He had seemed strangely friendly for a horrible German killer.

Perhaps, even now, they were working out the list. The list of the order in which they would . . . She braced herself. It was nonsense to think like that. She must be brave.

She looked about for a weapon.

Something heavy to bash at the first one, to make them see she would not submit without a fight.

Then she saw how badly that might go for her.

Would it be better just to submit? Just to lay back and let them get on with it? That way, at the least, she might not get herself hurt too much.

She sat on the bunk, her legs together, knees touching, feeling the tremble.

When heavy voices approached and she heard the harsh hateful German words she tensed up. Colour flooded her face and then receded, leaving her face pinched and white. She rubbed a hand through her hair. She forced herself to sit up straight, as she had been taught, and her breasts thrust at the grey shirt. Quickly, she pulled the leather jacket about her shoulders and tried to fasten it in front; but her shape made that difficult.

So, trembling, filled with despair and terror, Angelique Savinien awaited the first of the U-boat men to call on her.

'It's a problem, right enough, skipper.'

'Nothing we can't handle, Kern.'

'I don't think you mean what you might have said . . .'

Wolz decided not to become angry.

'We are officers and gentlemen of the Kriegsmarine. The hands will do as they are told. I don't think anyone will offer violence to the French girl. D'you know her name?'

'No, skipper. No one has been allowed near her. Ludwig is standing there like Hector.' Ehrenberger laughed. 'Reche was most disappointed he was not allowed to doctor the girl.' Ehrenberger told his skipper of the plans of the Sanitatsobermaat.

'We may need Reche yet. The girl must have gone through hell.'

'She looked in a daze, but, well, that is to be expected. But she looked – oh, you know, skipper. As though she was quite capable of handling the situation.'

'Yes. She thanked me. That's strange.'

Then the Number One brought up a subject that had caused Wolz a little concern for its implications.

'She's French. But which sort of French?'

'Only one way to find out. Call me if anything develops.'

'Very good!'

Going through the wardroom to the corner that, by reason of the green curtain was the captain's cabin, Wolz reflected that this whole situation was one he could well do without.

Thank God they were on their way back to Lorient! Suppose they'd picked the girl up at the beginning of the patrol. He pushed the thought aside as he pushed the green curtain aside after knocking on the usual metal panel. Riepold said: 'She seems all right, skipper. Nothing unusual happening.'

Nothing unusual!

Wolz went in and pulled the curtain shut.

The girl did not rise. She stared up at him and, with a sick feeling of despair, he recognised the terror in those luminously beautiful brown eyes.

'Please, mademoiselle,' he said in his best French, halting to find the right word, stumbling over the syntax. 'Please. You will be cared for properly. How do you feel?'

She had been given the cup of coffee Riepold had ordered. It had warmed for perhaps three minutes; now she shivered again.

'Schnapps,' said Wolz. 'I think, cognac? I think that is what the doctor would order for you now.'

She flinched back.

No idea of what might cause that flinching occurred to Wolz. She might be an enemy, she might not. How she regarded him he could only surmise; but she had thanked him.

He would have to box around this one very delicately.

He poured a small glass of schnapps, doled out with miserly concern in the boat, for spirits and good seamanship did not mix, and she sipped, making a face, coughing.

He spoke in his careful halting French and learned her name was Angelique Savinien. She would tell him nothing more. When he told her the name of the ship from which he had rescued her, she tossed her head, and remained silent.

The leather jacket did not meet at the front of the grey shirt. The curves he saw there, clearly outlined, reminded him of so many girls he had known. This Angelique was a real stunner. The leather coat had belonged to Gerhardt. He would not need it any more. He had been buried with due solemnity at sea. A stupid broken hoisting link had done for him.

And now this French girl sat sipping schnapps, wearing poor Jakob Gerhardt's leather coat.

He asked her various questions, trying to find out what had happened when *Belphegor* had been abandoned; but she would not answer. The experience had been too much for her, he surmised, and so, at last, he stood up and put his hand on the green curtain.

'You are perfectly safe here, Mademoiselle Savinien.

A man will stand duty outside at all times. We are on our way to Lorient – that should please you.'

She looked startled for a moment, then the set, white look settled on her face once more.

What the Gestapo would have to say to her when they did arrive at Lorient, he was not at all sure. They'd try to establish why she had been in the ship sailing to England. In all probability she was a good Frenchwoman and, realising the war was over, would be happy to co-operate like all the other French – at least, with the exception of those few idiots who seemed to think their war was still on.

He left her with: 'If there is anything you need, please ask. If it is possible –' He smiled. 'Well, we are rather – er – cramped in a U-boat.'

She did not thank him again.

Baldur Wolz went back to the bridge and the task of fighting the U-boat war against England.

CHAPTER NINE

When BdU signalled that official confirmation had come through that Oberleutnant Baldur Wolz had been awarded the Eisernen Kreuz, First Class, for his work in Narvik to add to the Second Class award of the Order he held for, he supposed, the escapade with U-42 and U-40, he authorised a small celebration.

Truth to tell, there was no holding Ehrenberger and Riepold, both of whom had received decorations. Privately, Wolz thought the whole thing redundant. Yes, they had done good work. But the Iron Cross Second class was a fraud, for despite all his work U-40 had not sunk *Ark Royal*. And, to cap that, although they had successfully brought U-55 out of Narvik, they had not sunk *Warspite*.

Loeffler had also been decorated. U-55 hummed with furious activity as they set about organising the celebration.

The machinists knocked up a facsimile of the Eisernen Kreuz from a flattened piece from a tin, and black paint and white paint, and they made a very handsome job. They made the cross with loving care for Daddy.

Wolz looked at it.

'That's twice as big as the real thing!' he protested.

But the hands insisted he wear it, at least, whilst they finished up this patrol. Then he could have the real thing.

Wolz said: 'I shall keep this, you may believe, with great sentiment.'

So they put the gramophone on and played all their records, and the familiar tunes held a new ring for them as U-55 ploughed her long way back across the grey Atlantic to their new home in Occupied France.

'You know, skipper,' said Ehrenberger, lolling back on the wardroom sofa, beaming, 'everyone will get a decoration after this cruise. And, it's certain you'll get the Ritterkreuz.'

'Maybe,' said Wolz. 'But we still have that last eel to dispose of.'

Number One waved a hand largely in the close air.

'We'll find a target, skipper. You'll see.'

'They'll have it painted on the conning tower before you have time to hang it around your neck.'

The thought gave Ehrenberger and the other officers in the wardroom great satisfaction. Neitzel stood bridge watch. Somehow – and just how Wolz wasn't going to make an enquiry – the celebration took place in the Third Officer's watch.

He was aware of the danger of alienating Neitzel; but he had already made up his mind that the well-being of his team meant more than the welfare of one man. That

6

had to be the cardinal rule. U-55 was beset with dangers from every direction, and only a team could bring her through. He fancied he would try to get rid of Neitzel. He might be lumbered with another useless officer; he did not think that very likely. Every now and then a bad apple showed up; he had been very lucky so far.

They had asked Mademoiselle Savinien to join them; she had refused.

The loss of his cabin meant little to Wolz, who spent most of his time on the bridge. The confidential documents and books had been transferred to the radio shack and locked away. His personal possessions were very few and the wardroom absorbed those. In a U-boat everything had to be left in the open because of space limitations. A man might be dying for a piece of chocolate, say, and the stuff lying there in full view. A good U-boat man never even considered the temptation. The property in a U-boat was either the property of all, or it was private. Either way, it was sacrosanct.

The supplies of sausages, like stalactites swinging from the overhead, were drastically thinned now. But rations were still good and adequate. The only real problem – apart from the French girl – was the starboard engine. And once they were safely in Lorient that would be attended to.

'Forty-nine three,' Riepold was saying. He said it two or three times.

'Only if that A.M.C. was fourteen,' said Wolz, determined not to allow any headiness into his feelings. But all the same! To be so close to the first magic target figure of fifty thousand tons! It was maddening as well as exhilarating.

'Bound to be, skipper.'

'Well,' said Riepold. 'The skipper could be right.'

'We could not make a positive identification, and you know how sticky they are over that. And the munitions ship might not be a full ten thousand. The book confirms it, but . . .'

'Now look on the bright side!' exclaimed Loeffler,

bustling in from the control room from which he would not be willingly absent for long, except to potter over his engines and damn the regulations. He was responsible in ways different from these sea officers, and his jargon was often arcane to them, shared mutterings with his engineers.

That shook Wolz right back to Marlene, preparing for her act, speaking to him with the bright brittle smile painted back on that face he had thought so much improved.

The schloss, well, that remained as always the same to him. It had been his home for as long as he could remember. And Marlene had seemed so bright, and now . . .

'What is it, Marlene?'

She dragged on her cigarette. Her fingers trembled. Her mouth trembled. She wore a bright red dressing gown, pulled tightly around her, sitting in the little room she used. The noise of the expectant guests sounded from the wide room with its fireplaces and chandeliers and tall curtained windows.

'That little tart Renate! She's making up to Siegfried – it makes me sick, Baldur. An empty-headed little bitch with a nasty way with her – she's got a figure like a snake – '

Wolz felt it would be impolitic to correct Marlene in her present mood. She had gone right back to that depressed, chain-smoking, drinking viciousness that had so disturbed him on their last meeting. But, all the same, Renate could not have a figure like a snake and have landed the job she had. Gurke at the theatre would only take on girls who were built right. That was his job, the way he made his money, and he was good at it.

Marlene laughed, a little too wildly for Wolz's comfort.

'By God, Baldur! You try to be good to me – I can't see why. You don't seem to want, and I'm here. It's all here, if you want it. Have you got some little Fraulein tucked away somewhere?' She shot it at him, rocking forward on her chair, staring at him accusingly. 'Some sweet innocent little thing, that – '

'No,' said Wolz. He spoke harshly, deliberately. He wasn't prepared to discuss Trudi with anyone, least of all Marlene, or so he thought. And, anyway, Trudi did not fit the description of the kind of girl Marlene had in mind.

She laughed again. 'So that's it.'

'No,' he said, again, evenly. 'No, Marlene. There is no sweet little Fraulein. And, as for you, I don't forget Siegfried.'

'No? Neither do I. But I think he will forget me if Renate gets her claws into him.'

After a few more words he tried to make reassuring, and Marlene's moody and somehow empty repetition of her words: 'Look on the bright side, I suppose,' Wolz left her to her final preparations and went back to the drawing room where the guests waited.

Siegfried met him with a slopping champagne glass.

'Now, then, Baldur! Where have you been hiding yourself?' Before Wolz could answer, a glass filled with his uncle's champagne was thrust into his hand, and Siegfried went on quickly: 'Come over here, cousin. I want you to meet Herr Doctor Dentz.'

He was shaking the hand of a small, plump, bespectacled man in an incongruous evening dress, like a penguin, but whose ice-chip eyes and thin bitter mouth promised surprises for anyone who assumed he was a penguin.

'U-boats?' said the Herr Doctor. 'Now I could tell you a few things about them.'

'But you won't, will you, Doctor Dentz.' And Siegfried laughed, and drank off his champagne quickly. 'Not on your life you won't.'

'You are correct, although I am sure the Herr Oberleutnant will understand. In a year, say, he will know far more about these things than he does now.'

Wolz's ears pricked up.

'If you can give us eels that work, Herr Doctor –'

'Ah! I have heard about that. An unsatisfactory

84

business. But your contact pistols should do the trick.'

'Oh, they'll explode all right,' said Wolz. 'If the depth mechanism works, if the steering goes right, if a hundred different things.' Then, quickly, he looked around.

'It's all right here, Baldur,' said Siegfried. 'We are all loyal party men, SS, Gestapo – you can trust everyone here.'

But Wolz knew he had said too much already. So he made himself smile and say: 'The Herr Doctor knows far more about all this than I do. All I can do is take my boat out and sink English ships.'

'The more the merrier,' said Doctor Dentz. And now he, too, laughed. The effect was that of a shark laughing. Wolz nodded, not too stiffly, and moved away. He was on leave and he wanted to get on with the things of leave; U-boats would always be there for him as long as the war lasted.

Then Cousin Manfred arrived, unexpectedly, bursting in with a group of fellow Luftwaffe officers, bringing a great splash of airforce blue into the black and red and white.

After the initial back-slappings and bellowed greetings subsided, and drinks had been handed around, the meeting was in the mood for Marlene's show.

'It'll be just the same, Baldur,' said Manfred, his blond hair immaculate, the Eisenkreuz on his breast pocket a marvel of shiny black and white, his face flushed. He looked his usual elegant self; yet about him there was a tenseness, and the lines were more deeply marked around his eyes and mouth than Wolz remembered.

For a space as the gathering quietened and men found places to stand or sit – and there were women there, too, now, laughing more shrilly than their menfolk, avid for a sensation – Manfred could talk easily to Wolz.

'You've been flying a lot lately, Manfred?'

'All day in the air. It's no secret. We've been over England. Challenging them to come up and fight us. But they don't – only when they have an advantage.'

Wolz sipped his champagne carefully.

He knew that Manfred would speak only of things he was allowed to mention.

'And so you've met the English Spitfire at last?'

Manfred nodded, and drank quickly, looking around for another glass.

'Yes.'

Not quite sure if he was saying the right thing, Wolz said: 'I trust you shot a number down.'

'Two – at least, one. One was a Hurricane.'

'Congratulations.'

'Oh, yes, congratulations. But they shot down Willi and Heinrich and little Peter . . . '

The second glass went down even more quickly than the first.

Wolz nodded.

'You never really get over seeing your comrades go. At least, I haven't, so far.'

'We will, Baldur, we will. It will become very familiar.'

The horror was that that was true.

'They gave me this.' Manfred touched the Eisenkreuz. 'It's a nice knick-knack.'

Wolz did not say anything; and the music blared and the curtains parted and the show began.

As the girls danced on to the polished boards at the end of the room, Manfred said, softly, quickly, into Wolz's ear: 'Trudi von Hartstein? She doesn't write any more.'

Wolz kept his face wooden. 'I know nothing.'

Then they looked as the girls went through their act.

With Marlene in the lead the girls went through contortions that were even more daring than before. The four girls were each dressed in a different fashion; but they all showed what they were made of. The women in the audience sat up a little straighter; but the men at their sides lapped it up, and so their companions reasoned out, not without a little self-satisfaction, that tonight would be all the more interesting for the show. That was one of its objects, of course.

Wolz stared with his usual honest interest, until he had

86

seen all he needed to see to resurrect the bright naked images before his mind's eye on the bridge of his U-boat in the thickest and dirtiest of nights off the western coast of England where the ships were to be snapped up.

Renate was not built like a snake, for her waist was narrow and her hips narrow also; but her breasts swelled and trembled as she danced. No, he could see what Marlene had meant. Renate moved with a sinuousness very alluring, her skin gleaming in the lights, her body contorting and moving voluptuously.

Wolz nudged Manfred.

'See that one, second from the left?'

'The one who looks as though she could throttle you to death? Well?'

'She was saying how much she admired the Luftwaffe. I think she'd had enough of the SS for a space.'

'Oh.'

'Her name is Renate. Beautiful in bed. I think you're home and dry there, cousin.'

'Well, well! She shows taste.'

Wolz looked around.

'I wouldn't say anything to Siegfried. Just move in.'

'I'll do that, Baldur. My thanks.'

'Don't thank me. Thank those Luftwaffe uniforms.'

So Wolz forced himself to watch the remainder of the show. The girls sang, and that was not too bad. He found himself thinking of Lottie and Heidi; but they were both away. He fancied a girl; but he did not fancy any of Marlene's friends. When the show finished, with the black straps being cast off and the girls whirling about, the lights gleaming from their skin where the powder had all vanished, leaving roseate pink expanses of flesh, he followed Manfred past the guests who were ready now to begin the serious drinking of the evening. Some of the girls would come back to do solo numbers. Manfred headed for the rear changing rooms.

Siegfried was there, smiling, very much the genial host in his heavy way, resplendent in his SS uniform.

'I say, Siegfried.' Wolz smiled, holding out the

champagne glass he had picked up on the way. 'You know you were telling me about the field operations of the SS? Well, I want to hear how you got on in France.'

Siegfried hesitated.

'The night's young, Siegfried. And Marlene –'

'Marlene will wait, I know. She'll always wait.'

'What about Eban Emael? Now, there was a marvel –'

The SS officer in Siegfried rose to the bait.

'Oh, yes, the Luftwaffe parachutists are very good; but we had our own, you know. And the way we cut through France! Did I tell you?' Siegfried was off. Wolz steered him into a quiet corner and settled down to listen.

Anyway, he wasn't doing this entirely for Marlene's sake. He was genuinely interested in hearing how the battles in France had gone. The Panzer forces fascinated him, now he was so deeply committed to the U-boats.

After some time in deeply technical conversation, Wolz saw Marlene crossing the room towards them. She wore a dress, an evening gown of deep lustrous green that was, in its own revealing way, even more shocking than her nude SS officer's rig. Instead of black straps, harsh and voluptuous against her skin, white and pink under the lights, the green revealed rather by half-concealing. Clever girl, commented Wolz to himself. She had made herself up carefully, concealing the smudges, lightening shadows. She looked ravishing.

When she reached them in their alcove, Wolz stood up, smiling.

'Hullo, Marlene. Siegfried has been telling me how he won the war.'

At Siegfried's suddenly flushed reaction, a bewilderment that Wolz could share and laugh at, he said, quickly: 'You know what I mean, Siegfried. I'm a U-boat man; but I think I envy you more than even Manfred. But, you cannot do everything in a war.'

'No. Where is Manfred, anyway?'

'Oh,' Marlene waved her hand very gracefully. 'He's around.' She shot Wolz a look. He kept his face bland.

'I'll run and get some more champagne.' He spoke brightly. He went off. He did not return to them.

Well, he said to himself, if Manfred doesn't make the most of it that is his look out. I'll not worry. But Marlene, now – she has her opportunity. For the sake of her health I hope she takes it.

He felt absolutely confident that Renate, wriggling her snake hips, pouting, thrusting out her chest to the best advantage, would respond in exactly the right way to Manfred. She might never have thought about the Luftwaffe; but he knew Manfred would steam in with all colours flying, and Renate – well, who knew what might come of that? One thing was sure, she wouldn't be fool enough to turn him down flat.

She wasn't the kind to make a mistake like that.

With abrupt and shocking suddenness the alarms rang violently through U-55.

The officers in the wardroom sprang to their feet.

A shouting, the heavy clatter of men's feet, the ringing of the iron treads of the conning tower ladder, the abrupt change of all routine.

'Flood! Dive! Enemy aircraft!'

Baldur Wolz broke from the wardroom racing for the control room, furiously angry with himself.

U-55 was under aerial attack, and here he was, lolling about in the wardroom celebrating his Iron Cross.

In the next few seconds he could be celebrating in a U-boat plunging helplessly through the water to utter destruction.

CHAPTER TEN

Flying Officer Matthews drove the big Sunderland at the pencil-streak of the U-boat in the water. The boat wallowed along ahead of them, going from port to starboard. The Sunderland was on the southerly leg of her patrol, near the limits of the prudent endurance line.

'Come on, Percy, come on!' said Matthews, urging the big boat through the air.

The four radials smashed out the power and the props churned the air. The Sunderland was flat out. Up in the front Nash and Thompson turret Sergeant Timmins wanted to open fire; but at the range he knew his .303s would never reach. Flight Sergeant Rowlandson in the bomb aimer's position stared narrowly through the sights. Come on, come on, Percy, he was saying to himself, over and over. The skipper had picked up the best course he could. They'd broken out of light cover to see the U-boat in front of them, steaming along as though the sea belonged to the bastard. Now they were lumbering down as fast as they could, the Sunderland thrashing through the air like a runaway railway train.

With bombs loaded they had to score a direct hit. The Navy had depth charges; but this Sunderland was equipped with bombs, and even the R.A.F. depth charges were somehow or other not scoring the kills they should.

Wide-winged, engines roaring, the Sunderland screamed towards the U-boat.

White water foamed about her. Spurts of white rippling all along her hull.

'She's diving!' screamed Rowlandson into his mike.

'I've lost her,' said Matthews. Up in the driver's seat

he had lost the U-boat beneath the Sunderland's bulky hull. 'Keep on track – '

The sun shone over the Sunderland's tail. They'd only just turned north from their southerly leg. Another few minutes and they'd have missed the sub.

'She's going, skipper!'

'Come on, come on!'

The Sunderland pulled flatly out of that screaming dive, as steep and as fast as Matthews dared make it. The sea below them foamed and spread in a white circle of suds. Rowlandson held the sights on . . . on . . . on . . . He pressed the tit.

'Bombs gone!'

Flying Officer Matthews swung the big boat in a wide-winged arc, banking around. Now he could see. The swirling disturbed water where the U-boat had dived, and then the smaller, bursting white eruptions of his bombs. They must have been triggered by the disturbance in the water. He did not think they had hit the U-boat.

He circled. Everyone who could glared down upon the surface of the sea.

Nothing.

No debris, no oil slick – nothing.

'A frost, chaps,' said Matthews.

He felt the sick bitterness that they had been too late. But even he, with all his love for Percy, knew that a Sunderland had to catch a U-boat with its pants down to sink it with a direct hit from bombs. And the chap on the bridge down there had been slow. No doubt of it. Another two or three minutes and they'd have nailed him.

Resignation in his voice, Matthews spoke into the intercom.

'We did it all right, chaps. Nice show. Pity there's nothing to show for it at the end.'

Still feeling the nagging despair that rode him like an ulcer, he turned the Sunderland on course, flying back home, knowing he would get there with a few pints of high octane in the tanks. What a lousy war this was!

The concussions as the bombs exploded in the disturbed water scarcely affected U-55. She plunged deep. Neitzel had given his orders in panic, and the boat dived and dived deep.

He had been thinking of the French girl's shape and of what he would like to do, and exchanging a few words with von Magdorf on totally unrelated subjects, knowing the mid shared his opinions about girls like the French girl. She was ripe for it. That was clear. All French girls were the same. Everyone knew that.

The lookout had yelled the moment he'd swung his glasses towards the sector where the Sunderland vectored in on them. There were scattered clouds there; but they were behind and higher than the flying boat. She should have been spotted a deal earlier than she had been.

Even as he shrieked his orders and the boat began to dive, Neitzel had worked out his excuses. Clearly, as officer of the watch it was his duty to keep the men up to their work. But one man had been late. He must take the blame, for Neitzel did not intend to do so.

He would blame an old wound. He had been hit slightly on the forehead by a rebounding chunk of wood from the garbage scow. Yes, that had caused him severe headaches, and just for that moment he had not been watchful enough. In that brief moment the Sunderland had pounced, and the lookout had failed. Yes, that was what he would say to this devilish Oberleutnant Wolz.

That devil himself burst into the control room and the icy look of rage on his face chained the duty personnel to their instruments. Loeffler was there, like a stage genie always popping up when needed. Wolz's rage was all for himself. Neitzel slid down the conning tower ladder last.

Wolz ignored him, bent beneath the maze of piping to glare at the depth indicators.

They were diving fast.

They shot through fourteen, twenty, twenty-five, fifty metres like a shell from a gun. At a hundred metres, with the explosions above them mere memories, Wolz said: 'Level out, Chief. Blow bow.'

Loeffler gave his orders. U-55 slowed her manic descent.

The thump of the pumps, the low thrilling purring of the electric motors, all sounded strange after their long absence. At a hundred metres U-55 slid through the waters.

Wolz stepped back and straightened. He turned to Neitzel.

'I take it the aircraft was very close, Herr Leutnant.'

Neitzel found it extraordinarily difficult to look directly at his commander.

'Yes, Herr Oberleutnant.'

'I see. Lookouts?'

'The aircraft broke from cloud. She was on us before we had a chance to – '

'Why type was the aircraft?'

'Sunderland.'

'I see.'

One thing Wolz was not going to do was give Neitzel a dressing-down or a tongue-lashing before the men. A lot of commanders did that. Wolz had observed how this was a thing his English friends did not much care for and avoided whenever possible. The fellow in the Sunderland had given them a fright. But they were all right. They'd dived to safety.

'I'll see you in my cabin later, Herr Leutnant.'

'Very good!'

Maybe, as had been suggested to him before, he was over-influenced by his stays in England. He got on well with some of the English. They seemed to feel sorry for him, and always expressed their sympathy when they learned his father's U-boat had been run down by a German vessel. But he had not missed the English antipathy, hatred and fear of even the word U-boat. Even Dick Mitchell shared a great deal of that feeling, and Mitchell had served in British submarines later on, after Wolz had returned to Germany. What he was doing now, God alone knew. Wolz did not think he was in the Sunderland that had nearly got them.

When he was assured the U-boat was functioning perfectly, Wolz decided to come up to the surface in exactly one hour. It might be a useful corrective to the crew to make them realise again, and forcefully, that U-boats dived below the surface. They had spent so much of this patrol on the surface a little diving stations routine would not come amiss.

He went along to see how Angelique Savinien was taking the fuss, and found her lying on the bunk, rigid, her hands together. Her face was very white.

'There is nothing to fear, mademoiselle. One of your late allies paid us a visit. That is all.'

Midshipman Johann Henke stood guard at the green curtain. His brightly-scrubbed pink face regarded his commander with a look whose implications were not lost on Wolz. The youngster was very keen, which was excellent; but Wolz fancied there was a deal too much hero-worship for this rakish U-boat skipper under whom he served for the good of Wolz's soul. He hated having to cut the mid down to size – in fact had only had to talk hardly to him once. Otto von Magdorf, the other Fahnrich, was a bit of a boil by comparison.

'No trouble here, mid?'

'None, Herr Oberleutnant. The lady remains very quiet.'

'Well, it is all very strange to her. She's not used to U-boats like you and me.'

'No. That is right, Herr Oberleutnant.'

Smiling to himself, Wolz went back to the control room.

The mid had acted well during the affair of the garbage scow, too. There they'd been, carrying out the last of the seemingly eternal practice runs, loaded up with a full kit of torpedoes, chugging along to pick up their wires and berth discreetly alongside the other training U-boats.

Only Wolz knew from a commander-only cypher that their training had been cut short and they were to go on ops. He'd been on the bridge with Ehrenberger and Henke and Riepold, bringing U-55 in sweetly. Around them the training base presented its usual somewhat distraught air of impending panic. The sun was sinking over the island and the light lay in long golden streaks upon the calm water. Opposite, on the other bank, the blacked out wharves showed as dark streaks, with boats tied up there. A tug chugged sedately along the centre of the anchorage taking a fifty ton garbage scow out.

They had been carrying out a practice patrol right up to the final moment when, having sighted a target and got the sights on, the order to loose would be given.

The light glanced from the waters, making a bright dazzlement. The shadows of the far bank looked even more deeply bruised by contrast.

Gently, U-55 swung in towards the mooring wires. Wolz eyed the tug and the barge and the easy calculation flowed in his mind that they would be well past and clear before U-55 was anywhere near them. At the moment they were at least a thousand metres away.

'Permission to come on the bridge!'

That was the Third Officer.

'Come on up, Herr Leutnant.'

Wolz was perfectly prepared to relax the strict sea discipline now they had finally worked-up and were safely within their training anchorage.

Neitzel climbed up the ladder and stood on the bridge, looking out at the sunset. He breathed deeply. Wolz felt a curiosity if the lieutenant did not care over much for the stink of a U-boat. Wait until he had spent a patrol out beyond Finisterre, and then he might think about complaining.

'All secure below, Herr Leutnant?'

'All secure, Herr Oberleutnant.'

U-55 ghosted gently along, the ripples passing from her sharp bow down her flanks, spreading widely past her bulging saddle tanks. Her grey steel was fresh and bright.

Everything had been put back in place in apple-pie order after her ordeal up the fjord at Narvik.

U-55 thumped and the hiss of compressed air and the string of bubbles told Wolz exactly what had happened.

There was nothing anyone could do now.

U-55 lifted as the weight loss of the torpedo was not compensated for by the Chief's flooding.

Shouts lifted. Wolz grabbed the loud-hailer and bellowed forrard. But, as everyone knew, nothing could be done and destiny must take its course.

The wake of the eel showed, a milky glimmering tinged with orange across the ripples of the anchorage.

'Anyway,' said Riepold. 'The eels aren't armed.'

'They were for the exercise,' said Neitzel.

'What!' He was the centre of an astonished battery of accusing eyes.

'It was laid down – anyway – '

'Anyway,' said Riepold, determined to be optimistic as the torpedo shot away from the U-boat. 'The thing won't work. Or it'll sizzle. Or it'll circle.'

Yes, said Wolz to himself, the rotten torpedo won't work. Please God it doesn't!

But, of course, it did.

The column of white water lifted at the side of the refuse barge. The sunset glowed orange and crimson all along the side of the column of upflung water. The barge lifted. It reared. It broke in two and scattered into a thousand fragments. The tug surged ahead, belted along by the blast and the shock wave of roiling water. U-55 heaved.

'Get below, Kern, and find out the idiot who did it!' bellowed Wolz when they could hear again.

Ehrenberger vanished down the hatch.

'I didn't – ' began Neitzel.

'Not now, Neitzel. Later.'

U-55 slid forward into the spreading mass of debris. It stank.

Bits of planking, refuse, decayed cabbages, potato-peelings, offal – all manner of disgusting refuse swam in the calm waters and bumped the boat's plating.

The whole anchorage gradually became choked with garbage.

The enquiry was strange. The gravity of the situation was without doubt. But a hidden levity possessed the officers, and the U-boat was needed at sea in the front line, and the smell hung about for days, anyway. In the event, the torpedo man who had leaned on the trigger without knowing the torpedo release gear was all set got off with a severe reprimand. No one could explain why the trigger had not been set to safe, why the whole thing was live in the first place.

A black mark went up against the skipper of U-55. But at the same time his boat got a name that, he knew with moody dejection, would most likely stick.

The muck-spreader. That was U-55's name in the U-boat arm of the Kriegsmarine.

The muck-spreader.

Sometimes they were not as polite as that.

It occasioned great mirth.

The whole crew of U-55 was glad to get away from the training base and get to sea. And, most of all, her skipper . . .

'I'll give 'em muck-spreader,' said Wolz to himself as, at last, he gave the orders to surface. 'I'll show 'em with forty thousand and more tons!'

Sanitatsobermaat Reche felt the disgruntlement within him as a physical hurt. He was a valuable man in the boat. Everyone knew that. He knew it. He had to deal with all kinds of injuries and sicknesses, and he'd had a skimpy course that was supposed to make him as competent as a Herr Professor Doktor. He twirled a tin of ointment between his fingers, moodily, thinking.

It was always the same. As soon as a fellow was hurt they yelled for Reche. Poor Jakob! Gerhardt had been squashed flat, squashed like a trodden-on beetle. All his insides had squeezed out. It was horrible. And they'd calmly sent for Reche to come with a bucket and clean

Z

up. And Waldemar! His foot had been crushed and so they'd expected Reche to cut his toes off and save him from gangrene.

It was all too much.

The officers had all the fun. They'd got that French piece in there and were having the time of their life – and he wasn't asked to attend to her. Oh, no! He'd heard them, whooping it up, with the gramophone blaring, and laughing and drinking and shouting, and who knew what the French piece was letting them do behind the green curtain.

They'd been so engrossed they'd nearly got old U-55 sunk by a rotten English aeroplane.

Reche stood up. U-55 had surfaced and now nosed along through the swell. The weather would worsen before it got better as autumn gave way to the beginnings of winter.

'That girl needs me to care for her,' he said to himself. There was no privacy in a U-boat. But Reche was able to go through to the wardroom without attracting attention, requesting permission to move about applied when they were trimmed off submerged.

The Chief stood in the control room superintending his maze of dials and soon he'd take one of his routine looks into the engine room. U-55 only had one engine left, now, and Reche blamed the officers for that. The skipper and the two mids and Riepold were on the bridge. Ehrenberger stood in the control room talking to the Chief. Reche pushed through to the wardroom, carrying his tin of ointment.

Neitzel looked up. 'Yes?'

'Beg to report duty as Sanitatsobermaat, Herr Leutnant.'

Neitzel looked puzzled.

'I'm the only one here and I'm all right, Reche.'

'It's the girl,' said Reche with great confidentiality. He ducked his head at the green curtain. 'She must have been injured. I have to rub my ointment in where it will do the most good. It's a matter of honour.'

Neitzel felt the wave of lust flash through him, and then the calculation. He was under no illusions about the way he was regarded by the officers of U-55.

'If you have Daddy's permission, then proceed, Reche.'

'Very good!'

Reche moved confidently towards the green curtain. Neitzel threw down the magazine and stood up. Silently, he followed the Sanitatsobermaat.

For Angelique Savinien the knowledge that the submarine was really and truly swimming under the water filled her with a dread she could hardly understand. She found it hard to breathe. The air tasted foul, flat and metallic and loaded with stinks. The stench of sweaty male bodies made her feel faint. The heavy perfumes made her want to vomit.

She lay on the bunk rigid. Her nightdress was still damp, and even the clothes she wore clung wetly to her. It had grown appreciably colder.

The green curtain parted and a chunky, sweating German appeared. He smiled. She started to sit up; but he put a hand on her forehead in a professional way, gabbling in harsh German. She did not understand him, but he had a tin of ointment in his left hand. He smiled again. There was a strange shiny look about his face, and the sweat ran down past his nose. His eyes looked ... Angelique tried to sit up again, gasping, and the man's thick fingers wrenched her grey shirt open.

'No! No – what?' she cried, struggling.

He pushed her flat. What he said she did not know; but it did not sound hard. Weirdly, it sounded as though he wanted to be helpful, although she could not be sure.

His fingers dug out ointment. He began to rub the stuff over her shoulders. He pushed the shirt down. Angelique made a movement to pull the shirt up; but the man's strength overcame her resistance. The shirt split and ripped down and she was bare to the waist. The German sailor dolloped a huge chunk of ointment between her breasts, began to rub it in, round and round, massaging, fondling her breasts, tweaking her nipples. His hand slid lower.

'No!' shouted Angelique. 'This is not –'

In passable French, another German spoke from where he stood in the parted green curtain.

'Rest quietly, mamselle. This is for your own good. It is necessary in a U-boat.'

'Necessary?'

'But assuredly, yes. It will prevent the cold. Slip your trousers off. Let the – let the attendant rub the ointment well in all over. You will thank us.'

Angelique did not know what to think or do. So far she had been treated with respect. Her fears had been proved groundless. But, her breasts, flaunted naked for these men to see – and now they wanted her to take off her trousers . . .

Neitzel moved into the cramped cabin and bent down. He smiled at the girl. He put his fingers on the belt and heaved the buckle open.

'Pull them off, you fool,' he said to Reche.

The ends of the trousers were gripped in Reche's greasy fingers. As he pulled, so Neitzel lifted Angelique's nude body. The coarse trousers slid down. Neitzel let out an exclamation. He was raging. Angelique saw his face, his eyes, and she knew . . .

She screamed.

'No, no, mamselle. We will not hurt you . . .'

Neitzel was all over her now. His hands rubbed ointment into her skin, feeling the softness of the flesh, the hardness of her nipples, rubbing and caressing. He reached down and laved the ointment over her stomach, moving in long slow rotund movements, reaching down.

Angelique screamed again and tried to struggle up and Neitzel put an elbow across her throat.

Reche was rubbing her shins and knees and thighs, crooning, saying, over and over: 'This will help you, lady. They should have asked me before. They don't understand what I have to do. But I know my duty.'

100

Neitzel was almost beyond control. He was rigid. He caressed the body of the girl, feeling the smooth glistening slide of his palm and fingers of his left hand along the curve of her stomach, his right hand bent and fondling her breast. He panted. His face was scarlet.

Then – and he never knew why – he sensed danger.

Instantly, in his passable French, he exclaimed: 'Mamselle! This is terrible!' And, in German: 'You filth! Get away! Get away!'

He grabbed Reche by the shoulder and spun him from the girl. He saw her body outspread, the length of her legs shining with ointment in the light, the darkness of shadow, the way her breasts trembled as she tried to struggle.

He threw Reche to the floor and stood over him, and so lifted his face and stared into the vicious eyes of Oberleutnant Baldur Wolz.

CHAPTER ELEVEN

The court of enquiry convened in the wardroom of U-55.

The President, Oberleutnant Wolz, sat flanked by Leutnant Ehrenberger and by Leutnant Loeffler. The bridge watch was being taken by Riepold and the mids, the feldwebels were handling the control room and engine room and were perfectly trustworthy. Neitzel faced the court, and Mademoiselle Angelique Savinien sat to one side, the tears still streaking her face, her clothes once more on but with the ointment still glistening on her skin.

'Now it's there,' Wolz had said. 'Best to leave it.'

Two men in the forward mess flat watched Sanitatsobermaat Reche. He sat shaking his head, and laughing a little, and saying: 'I showed them. I did my duty. They can't have all the fun to themselves and leave all the dirty work to me.'

The facts in the case were rapidly established. The trouble was, there were two sets of facts.

There was no dissent from the fact that Reche had cracked. He had flipped his lid. That was no novelty in the U-boat arm and there was always the chance that he would recover. Recuperative therapy would be employed back in Germany and, perhaps, he might wind up in an infantry unit of the Army. He would not be taken back into the Kriegsmarine. Wolz felt pretty certain of that.

Fact two was the attempt by Reche to minister to the French girl. Wolz privately felt that Reche imagined he was doing his duty, was helping, and that sexual pressures, although they were at the bottom of it all, were not paramount in Reche's mind. That he might have moved on to an actual criminal assault was not to be denied.

Then the two sets of facts differed.

Angelique Savinien said that the Herr Leutnant had also abused her, treating her indecently. He had intended – and here her hands went to her face, and her shoulders shook. It was not an act on her part. She had been frightened very badly. Wolz, coming down to the wardroom, had been only just in time, according to Mademoiselle Savinien. She was persuaded to speak only after a great deal of patient and thoughtful consideration on Wolz's part.

The other set of facts came from Neitzel. Reche had told him the skipper had ordered him to attend to the French girl. Only a sense that things were not quite right had brought Neitzel past the green curtain in time to see Reche beginning an indecent assault upon the girl. Rubbing ointment in was one thing. After all, to a medical man, men's or women's bodies were merely bodies for attention, and he, Neitzel, thought that they had all seen enough women's bodies for the sight to be commonplace. There was no room for privacy in a U-boat. But he had been suspicious. He was only happy that he had managed to stop Reche before the man had gone any farther.

Wolz looked at Neitzel, and at Angelique Savinien. It boiled down to belief in their word.

There seemed to him to be a distasteful aspect to this quite apart from the whole sorry shambles itself.

He was bound to take the word of a serving officer, an officer in the U-boat arm of the Kriegsmarine, against that of a silly little French girl who, so the authorities at home would say, was no better than she should be.

Always, with women in a boat, trouble accrued . . .

A little silence developed. Everyone looked at Wolz, either openly or covertly, waiting.

At last he spoke.

'The matter will be fully reported and no doubt a further enquiry will be held. For the moment I place it on record that it is hard to believe that a German Officer could be guilty of the actions described. The matter of the Sanitatsobermaat will be taken up separately. Therefore it is my ruling that the mademoiselle shall be confined to quarters and the guard upon her will be doubled. This will cause hardship in the boat. But I will not have a repetition of this disgraceful episode. The honour of the German Navy cannot be allowed to be tarnished in any way.'

And, he reflected, whilst that might let Neitzel off the hook, he had formed his opinion of Angelique and he felt he now knew about Neitzel. The man might be speaking the truth. But he was reprieved for the moment only because Wolz needed him carrying out his duties and not under close arrest. A U-boat was no place to have an officer under arrest. Once they reached Lorient and he could make his report, the authorities would handle the affair. Then, Wolz would be free to act as he wished he could act now.

That he might easily be construed as taking the

103

coward's course could not move him. U-55 and the welfare of her crew must come first. Even, temporarily, at the expense of a young and frightened and very beautiful French girl.

The bellow from the bridge came as a respite.

'Object off the port bow!' Then, moments later as Wolz reached the ladder and started up the conning tower: 'A boat. Ship's boat. Survivors.'

A brisk westerly wind stung Wolz's face as he climbed through the hatch on to the bridge. He turned his back on the breeze and peered ahead. A ship's lifeboat scudded along under a lug sail, white water breaking away in a creamy wash from her bows. U-55 ghosted along after, catching up. The people in the boat saw the U-boat and, realising any escape was useless, hauled in the sail. As far as Wolz was concerned they had nothing to fear from him. He just hoped they might give him information. Every scrap of news was vital in the continuing war in the Atlantic.

U-55 made a lee and the lifeboat eased in alongside. The men fending her off from the U-boat's saddle tanks looked fit enough. They moved with energy and did not show signs of exhaustion, which might be expected after days in an open boat.

A rope was flung and belayed.

Wolz peered down. He wondered what they were thinking in the boat. He looked down on them. They looked up. Their ship had been torpedoed by an unseen steel shark; and now they were close to a real live monster of the deep. The situation was not lost on Baldur Wolz. In their position he would be feeling a few odd thrills shooting through him.

The boat heaved up and down, fended off the saddle tank. There were women in the boat, their long hair flying from beneath a strange collection of hats. There were children also.

War was hell.

A few shouted enquiries and, not without a few smothered blasphemies from the boat, they said they

104

had been torpedoed and to hell with him and they wouldn't tell him the name of the ship and why couldn't you stinking Germans fight an honest war, and so on. Wolz refrained from comment.

'Do you have everything you need?'

'Yes, no thanks to you, you murdering Hun!' The steersman shouted up. He had taken the tiller to conn the boat over the last few tricky metres. He sported four gold rings on the blue sleeve of his monkey jacket. His hair was white.

'Water? Food? Maps? Compass?'

'We don't need a compass with this wind.'

'Mid,' said Wolz to Johann Henke. 'Nip below and fetch up one of the compasses. You know the ones. Smartly, now.'

When Henke had gone, Wolz bellowed down: 'I am sending you a compass. Your captain is to come aboard.'

The party Riepold led on to the forward casing carried MP 38 machinepistols. They would not be needed. But Wolz was in no mood to waste time. The first sight of authority – which was clearly and brutally represented by the machinepistols – would be enough. The captain scrambled aboard with a line about him. His red face ran with water, his hair was soaked; but he glared defiantly enough at Wolz as he was brought up on to the bridge.

'You murdering Huns! You ought to –'

'I am sure, captain,' said Wolz in his English-accented English, with no trace of a Germanic taint to it. 'But war makes us do things for which we may have regrets.' Henke appeared with the compass. 'Thank you, mid. Now just nip down again and tell the French girl to gather her belongings and come on deck. And bring some chocolate. I think we can spare some. And some schnapps.' He swung to Ehrenberger. 'You'd better superintend that little task, Kern.'

'Very good, skipper.'

The two shinned down the ladder.

Wolz turned to the master.

105

'I have a passenger for you.' The decision had been taken of itself. This would solve his problems. There was no doubt whatsoever in his mind now that Angelique Savinien had not only spoken the truth about Neitzel but that she was not one of this kind of Frenchwoman; but one of the other kind, the kind who was on passage to England and not France. That had been obvious from the first, anyway, only he and his officers had chosen to ignore its implications. The safety of his boat came first. There would be no trouble justifying this decision.

'Passenger?' The master gaped at him, taken completely by surprise.

There were about twenty people in the lifeboat, and Wolz estimated she had been designed to carry fifty, so there would be room enough. One of the seamen was a Negro, a huge black man, who looked cold, wrapped in an old blanket coat. Of the women and children, he felt they were in not too bad a condition. There seemed to be ample tarpaulins and the oars were all there and unbroken. The sail looked new, although the lifeboat had a few knocks and splinters in the gunwales.

'A passenger, captain,' repeated Wolz.

The master suddenly laughed.

'I get it! Rats deserting the sinking ship.'

Wolz checked his anger. He suddenly thought he understood about the children.

'No, captain. As you will see. But I assume you were on your way to America. Aren't your passengers rats deserting the sinking ship of England?'

The master's face flushed. He half lifted a meaty fist.

'Why, you dirty Hun, I'd like to –'

'Here you are, skipper!' shouted Ehrenberger. He pushed forward holding the bottle of schnapps. He was followed by Henke assisting Angelique to negotiate the hatchway.

'Here is your passenger, captain. Mademoiselle Angelique Savinien.' Abruptly Wolz was struck by the horrific thought of what the girl would say about her

106

experiences in his boat. He went on harshly: 'She will tell you that she has been well-treated, except for one regrettable occurrence. Believe me, captain, the man responsible will be severely punished. The lady has come to no harm. That I can vouch for.'

'So you've been up to your tricks again, have you?' The master took a look at Angelique. His craggy face softened. 'Why, she's no more than a girl, and scared witless by the look of it. What have you scum been up to?'

Again Wolz had to force himself to hold on to his temper.

He gestured for Henke to take Angelique down on to the fore casing. Half-turning back like that, he saw von Magdorf openly leering on the girl.

'Herr Midshipman von Magdorf!' he bellowed.

That was enough.

Von Magdorf swung back to his sector and began scanning sea and sky with marked application.

Angelique walked along the casing in the shoes they had given her, wadded with old socks. She clutched the Kriegsmarine blanket about the leather coat, and in her hand she held a bar of chocolate. She was in a daze. These fearful Germans were casting her adrift in a boat on the cruel sea. She could not quite understand the captain of the submarine. His name, she had heard, was Wolz. Baldur, the other officer called him. Somehow she was being transferred into the little lifeboat, getting wet again; but not too badly, slumping down on the floorboards where a gigantic black man, with a great smile, helped her to rise and sit upon a thwart.

'You'll be all right now, missy,' he said. She half understood, for her English was of the most rudimentary kind.

The master took the bottle of schnapps.

He said: 'Well, I'll not say that's not kind of you, captain. And for the compass. No doubt we'll reach land safely. I wish I could say I wished you the same.'

'I quite understand.' Wolz let himself smile. He saw Angelique looking up at him, and he touched his white commander's cap to her. 'The lady comes from *Belphegor*. I am afraid we were under the necessity of sinking her – after her crew deserted her and the lady. You may ask her. Now, captain, bon voyage.'

The master went back to his lifeboat without another word.

His thoughts, clouded, struggled to make him think that perhaps some of these Nazi rats weren't as bad as some others.

U-55 plunged on through worsening weather. The year looked as though it was going to end in violence after the long hot summer. The equinox would bring up the gales, right enough.

Wolz found himself thinking of Angelique Savinien and hoping the fragile lifeboat in which she sailed would reach land safely. Or, perhaps, the boat might be sighted and her passengers taken off by a British ship. If the ship was travelling westwards then Angelique might find herself once again in a sinking ship. The thought that a person might endlessly shuttle backwards and forwards across the Atlantic amused Wolz, until he saw into the darkness of the thought, at which all his amusement vanished.

He just wanted to sink ships and stop the English from carrying on the senseless war. He had no desire to sink ships filled with women and children. His job was to win the war his way, and the quicker he did it the better. That meant tonnages sunk.

Some other people he knew did not share that view.

That boil of an oaf, Kapitanleutnant Adolf Forstner of U-45, had been the kind of man Wolz would never dream of bothering his head about in the normal course of things. He stood in his corner of the bridge as the grey seas raced by and reflected that his decision not to wait for the Kapitanleutnant but to take off for Narvik had been very wise. It had brought him U-55 to salvage, to fight, and eventually to command. Also, it had brought him the implacable and bitter enmity of

Forstner. Forstner had achieved command in the U-boat arm through some chicanery. That seemed clear to Wolz.

After the contretemps with the garbage scow, they'd called in at Kiel for final orders. Coming back to the boat after a briefing that had filled him with an elation at the prospects ahead, Wolz had walked along the waterfront in something of a daze.

The blackout was rigidly enforced. The boats lay out there waiting for their skippers. The muted noise of the seaport reached him, a little breeze flicked his long coat around his legs, he held his brief case under his arm; he felt wonderful. On the morrow he would slip wires and head out into the Atlantic, hunting English ships.

Then the three dark figures had loomed up.

He could not see them very well.

One said in a hateful voice he recognised: 'So the Herr Oberleutnant is now a commander of a boat!'

Another harsh voice grated: 'I think he needs to be taken down a peg.'

The third man did not speak but leaped at Wolz.

Purely out of instinct Wolz jumped sideways and swung the briefcase in a flat arc. The leather case hit the man on the side of the head. Unfortunately for the fellow, in the case reposed a heavy chunk of machined steel, a valve-fitting the Chief badly needed for the number three pump.

With an explosive gasp like a breaking boiler, the man collapsed sideways.

Wolz was now fully alert. The greasy cobbles made footing difficult; but he angled sideways and put a foot into the second man's guts, following that up with a fist into his mouth. He felt teeth break and the warm wetness running over his knuckles. His hand stung and he just hoped he had broken nothing. If he had . . . The thought made him annoyed.

'I don't know you or who you are,' he shouted. He said the words very carefully, for he had no wish for Forstner to make more of this. 'But the police will have you by the heels for this.'

He jumped in. Forstner was suddenly trying to run away.

Wolz kicked him up the backside, gripped a collar and swung the briefcase at the Kapitanleutnant's head. If he killed the bastard he wouldn't mind, not in the mood he was in.

Forstner started to scream and the Chief's valve slugged into his head, and he pitched headlong to the cobbles.

Wolz stood over the three recumbent bodies. He kicked them a few times; but they did not respond. So, cursing them, as he was not at sea, he went off. He felt no elation, only a great sadness and the vindictive determination that if the oaf Forstner tried to make anything of this he'd have his guts out and strangle the boil with them.

CHAPTER TWELVE

When Wolz moved back into his cabin, one of the personal possessions he was most careful about was his Walther P38. The automatic had been given to him by Cousin Siegfried. By reason of his privileged position in the SS, Siegfried had managed to lay hands on a few of the guns issued for trial purposes before general issue. That was due for mid 1940, so Wolz understood. Siegfried, also, had allowed Marlene to use the straps, belt and automatic in her act, the holster being of a non-regulation kind, for the holster always seemed to follow on after the gun in military service.

If Wolz had had the auto when Forstner and his thugs tried to beat him up on the dockside in Kiel he'd probably have tried to use it, so black had been his vindictive mood. The blot! The boil! That a serving officer should hire two thugs to beat up a fellow officer proved almost impossible of belief to Wolz.

This was what came of having dedicated Party members in the Navy. Their first loyalty was to the Party and not to the Kriegsmarine. That kind of divided loyalty was not for Baldur Wolz, as it was not for most of his fellows. Gunther Prien, of U-47, the Snorting Bull of Scapa Flow, certainly was a Party member; but he had proved his worth as a fighting U-boat commander. Adolf Forstner had not.

Wolz had felt a tremendous elation in the company of commanders of U-boats who, he felt certain, would earn remarkable reputations very quickly now the Norwegian Campaign was over and the boats could return to the Atlantic. There was Otto Kretschmer – Smiling Otto, because he rarely did – of U-99. And Joachim Schepke of U-100. And Liebe of U-38 and Rosing of U-48. And Prien's old Number One, Endrass, of U-46.

He, Oberleutnant Baldur Wolz, could chalk up his scores alongside remarkable commanders of this calibre.

Now they were about to enter waters regularly patrolled by Coastal Command of the R.A.F. the lookouts must sharpen up still further the keenness of their watch. Soon Wolz would take U-55 below the surface and run during the day submerged.

The thought of that lone eel in the after tube itched at him. He ought to have loosed her off. Or he ought to have found another target by now; but BdU had ordered him back and he had received no orders from them to join an attack, nor had he picked up the radioed transmissions of another U-boat homing the pack on to a convoy.

Surely, on this course, before he vectored off for the run in to Lorient, he ought to sight an English vessel?

Surely?

*

111

At first the tiny dot on the horizon which lifted into view and then sank again beyond the sea rim meant nothing to the survivors in the longboat. The westerly still billowed their sail into a taut curve and the boat ran, thunking over the growing swell. Bad weather was due, and E. H. Collins, master of S.S. *Balintol*, broken to pieces now and sunk in the depths of the Atlantic, did not like the look of the sky.

'That is a ship, cap'n,' said Jonesy. His enormous white smile split his black face. Born in Liverpool, he had gone to sea as a youngster and had proved his worth. In the longboat he had proved a tower of strength. The women and children huddled under the tarps, for the weather was turning chilly.

'You're right, Jonesy,' said Pete McClellan, the Second Officer.

Suddenly, the people in the longboat realised what this meant.

A ship! Not a stinking U-boat but a real ship!

The flares went up sweetly.

Soon the dot grew in size and remained above the horizon. She came on, and turned into a sharp prow with two white wings. She made no funnel smoke.

'A warship,' said the master. Collins felt the thankfulness wash over him. Thank God! He had been dreading the days before him, with the women and kids in an open boat. The sea was already getting up. They were in for a blow. Now, suddenly, it was all going to be all right.

They waved and cheered as the ship raced up and then swung in a tight circle about them. She slowed. She was a trim little craft, low and lean, grey-painted, with a single funnel and a gun fore and aft. She bore a K pennant number and Collins felt choked up as he recognised the chance that had brought her to his succour in time.

Making a lee, the naval vessel secured the longboat alongside and the rope ladder went down and the hands willingly assisted the survivors inboard.

They came up, hauled and pulled, clutching their possessions, the children squeaking in an excitement liberated now they caught the vibrations from the adults and knew the dangers were over.

Leaning over his bridge, Lieutenant Commander Richard Algernon Mitchell kept his lean-jawed, smooth yet old-looking face grim. They called him a maniac – those who did not know him too well. He'd made Lieutenant Commander, much to his surprise, and been given H.M.S. *Cormorant* to play with.

That, at least, was how he had phrased it to his cronies. No one outside strictly Naval circles had ever heard of her. That was not surprising. At five hundred and ten tons she was a Patrol Sloop, built over at Fairfields in '35. Mind you, when you flashed her a quick look she looked, with her long rakish lines, like a destroyer. It was only when you looked more closely and saw how small she was, 234 feet between perpendiculars, that you smiled and nodded understanding.

But Dick Mitchell was proud of her with a deep and possessive pride. Her complement was well-salted with real Navy men, and the Hostilities Only ratings were being knocked into shape on the double. His Number One, Lieutenant Andy Stevens, was a bit of a stickler, and had been known to frown when the skipper roared up in his little MG, raising a dust along the dockside.

That, in a way, was the real gripe Mitchell had with his beautiful little *Cormorant*. Her turbines could churn out 3,600 horse power and that shoved her along at twenty knots. Not enough for a destroyer, not by a long chalk, and not nearly enough, Mitchell knew, when the confounded U-boats could do seventeen knots on the surface on their diesels.

'Get them inboard handsomely!' he roared, suddenly, as a girl stepped on to the deck, and staggered, and nearly fell until a leading seaman caught her arm to steady her. Mitchell looked at her. She wore a leather coat. That was odd.

Well, he'd get Number One to sort them all out.

The moment the longboat had been cleared he sent his command belting away. This was an area in which U-boats had been reported. Coastal Command had signalled through Naval HQ that they'd attacked one which got away. It was up to the Navy to go and find the elusive bastard in all this expanse of sea.

The tiny bridge thrummed as *Cormorant's* turbines built her speed up. Mitchell remained on the bridge. The asdic pinged away, and of echoes there were none.

Usually, in convoy, the asdic remained silent until action, for the U-boats were equipped with highly sensitive hydrophones and the sonic transmissions intended to trap them served only to attract them to their prey.

Like his fellows, Mitchell was learning the secrets and the knacks of fighting this sea war the hard way.

Presently Number One came up to the bridge. Andy Stevens presented a short, chunky, hard-bitten air. He would stand no nonsense from the crew and he would like to extend that hard practicality to his new skipper. Perforce, he did what he could to instil some of his own hard ideas of Naval discipline into the mixed bunch he had drawn as a crew. As for the ship, she was a jolly little number, with hidden quirks all her own; but he'd make of her a vessel to be proud of.

The breeze blew more strongly and the little sloop pitched and bucked as though to inform her new complement that she was a frisky little thing. White water burst over the narrow bows. The four-incher up there looked forlorn. The two-pounder aft was strictly non-regulation, and how Lieutenant Commander Mitchell had come by her, Stevens did not intend to enquire. Perhaps some of the skipper's rakish friends might know.

'All settling in okay, Number One?'

'They're mighty relieved to be rescued, I can tell you, sir. They're from *Balintol*, torpedoed on the outward run, so they're coming home unexpectedly. All except one.'

'The kids all right? What one?'

'They're eating it up. The steward's scrounged some duff for 'em. The blighters have got steel guts if you ask me. The one's a French girl – a real eye-opener. Came off a Jerry U-boat.'

'She did what!'

Lieutenant Stevens felt most pleased at the effect of his bombshell.

But, all the same, at the light in the skipper's eye, he hurried on.

'She was on the way to England, volunteered to be a nurse for the Free French chappies. Torpedoed. Says her ship was *Belphegor*. She's a bit distraught. Rambling on about the captain – '.

'The U-boat, Number One!'

'Yes, sir. Seems the crew abandoned ship prematurely, from what I can make out. She was left. She – '

'Left alone in an abandoned ship in the Atlantic! Good grief. Yes?'

'Then this U-boat hove up and took her aboard. I asked her the number; but she didn't know.'

'H'm. It sounds fishy to me. Does she speak German?'

'No. Well, she says not.'

'Well, I've a smattering. I'll give her a little test afterwards. If the Jerries intend to drop parachutists dressed as nuns on us, they can always drop a few Mata Haris in by U-boat, I suppose.'

'Yes, sir. Hardly likely, though – I mean – '

'Yes, Number One. Hardly likely.'

The lookout yelled then and every eye switched aloft. A Sunderland passed overhead, high, going towards the east. Mitchell sniffed.

'D'you suppose he saw us, Number One?'

'We're not all that small!'

'No. And we've a gun to prove it. All right, Number One. I'll come down and see this mysterious Mata Hari of yours.'

'Yes, sir. She's a real stunner.'

'Have her come to my cabin, will you?'

Aye aye, sir.'

In his tiny sea cabin – that by courtesy only – Mitchell prepared to play the devastating procurator general. The girl's story was so far-fetched that it probably had to be true. Anyway, Naval Intelligence would run her through the hoops and they'd come up with the right answers. The ship's corporal showed her in, and, with a somewhat lasciviously rolling eye, departed.

Mitchell stood up.

She *was* a stunner.

Speaking in his best German, as he had when that old devil Baldur and he had planned some of their most devastating larks in the old days, he said: 'And I believe you have something important you wish to tell me, fraulein?'

Angelique stared at the captain helplessly. Her deep brown eyes felt hot, smarting. She had been given a thick cup of a thick drink that had almost burned her lips. The sailors in their cheerful way had called it 'kai'. She had been able to wash and dry herself, although this ship seemed almost as wet as the lifeboat and the U-boat. She had brushed her hair, for a comb would not go near it. She had wiped her face. And now this mad Englishman was bellowing at her in what sounded like German.

Perhaps it was all a horrible trick. Perhaps this was really another German boat, brought here by the U-boat to capture them all. But that was impossible. She felt faint. She swayed.

Dick Mitchell watched her face. She was gorgeous. Despite the tough time she had gone through there was no mistaking the limpid clarity of those brown eyes, the perfect oval of her face, the lusciousness of the lips. The leather jacket – those beggars in the U-boat must have given her that – could not conceal that she was stacked to make a man's eyes bug out. She swayed. At once Mitchell took her elbow, guided her to the single chair.

'Sit down, sit down, mademoiselle,' he cried. 'At least,

116

you're not a Jerry. That's settled. There, there, it's all right now. We'll have you back home in a jiffy.' Then he realised what a fatuous remark that was. He felt astonishingly at a loss, he, old Ram Mitchell!

After a space Angelique had recovered sufficiently to answer a few of his questions with some coherence and repeat the story he had heard from Number One.

'Well, if this Capitaine Augier got back to England I'll have the blighter routed out, believe me! Going off and leaving a girl like you – it just won't do.'

His French was damned awkward; but she didn't have German and her English was a lot worse than his French. But, between them, they got along.

'And you didn't get the jolly old U-boat's number?'

'Non, mon capitaine.'

'A pity. Like to know who we're up against.'

'I am very tired, captain – '

'Yes, yes. Dashed thoughtless of me.' Mitchell fumbled around in French, expressing his contrition. 'Had to find out all I could. Duty, you know.' He helped her rise. She was a morsel. 'You'd best get off now and find out where Number One's stowed you.' Again the translation halted along lamely.

As she was going out, with no doubt as many men as could decently get themselves into positions of vantage to take the biggest eyeful they could, she said: 'No number, captain.' She spoke in her fractured English. 'No number. But zee captain his name. Yes. Yes. I hear that.'

'Oh?'

'His name – it was Wolz.'

Well, there must be a lot of Wolz's in Germany.

He opened his mouth to ask, and she said:

'Oberleutnant Baldur Wolz.'

'By God!' said Dick Mitchell. 'Old Baldy himself!'

The suspense was now over for the moment. BdU had signalled confirmations. Sources confirmed that H.M.S. *Archon* had been torpedoed and sunk. The AMC ran out

117

at thirteen thousand five hundred tons.

'Well,' declared Ehrenberger, defiantly. 'I said nearer fourteen than eleven, didn't I?'

'You said a lot more than that, Kern,' pointed out Loeffler. His gingery beard bristled in the merciless lighting.

Wolz laughed.

U-55 ran on sweetly. She had plenty of fuel left, in view of the salutary lack of requirements of the starboard engine. The food would last. He had got rid of Mademoiselle Angelique Savinien and, whilst he wished her the very best of luck, she could not count against the well-being of his crew. The only fly in the ointment was the charge hanging over Reche's head and the question mark over Neitzel's.

'With the confirmations, gentlemen, that makes it a grand total of forty-eight thousand eight hundred tons.'

'You'll probably have to take the AMC out of that and count her as a warship.'

'True, Kern. But, even so – '

'Even so,' bellowed Loeffler, excitedly, 'it's a tremendous score. And we've only just started.' Then his face screwed up. 'If it hadn't been for that crankshaft on the starboard diesel we'd be home now and kitting out with a fresh lot of eels. These Englanders don't really stand a chance.'

They all felt that, heady with the triumph of it.

'Just another measly twelve hundred,' said Ehrenberger. 'Just a little tramp, or a coaster straying out here. Something. Anything.'

The sighting alarm ripped the words asunder. Riepold, on the bridge, had sighted something. Wolz was barely aware of hurtling into the control room and of flinging himself up the ladder. He peered where Riepold pointed.

CHAPTER THIRTEEN

Lieutenant Commander Mitchell looked down past the blue-clad shoulder of the Pilot, Sub-lieutenant Tony Rookes, at the neat little crosses, the pencilled lines, and his lean face bore the frown of calculating concentration.

'The confounded thing is a right cock-up, Pilot,' he said. 'If the fly-boys got their navigation right, then we all need to go back to school.'

'We hit the three points it might have been, sir, dead on. The Sunderland wasn't at them. So they must have done their sums wrong.'

'And that mistake can cost them their lives.'

Diverted from the homeward leg to search for a downed Sunderland, *Cormorant* had scoured the area where, so it was claimed by Coastal Command, the Sunderland had gone in. The visibility was excellent between patchy drifts of a scudding rain that, after the incipient gale had taken off, promised the real blow to come. The waves boiled in from the Atlantic and drove against the thin steel plating. The turbines let rip with their intoxicating whirring power. The little sloop knifed through the seas. But all this power and energy and the keen lookout aloft could not locate the missing flying boat.

Mitchell tapped the chart thoughtfully. There was just room for the Pilot and himself in what was called the Charthouse.

'Use that think-tank of yours, Pilot. What's the sort of mistake their navigator would have made in an aeroplane coming down on the sea – in a hurry, his position problematical – who knows when he last got a decent sight?'

The Pilot had landed his job and the rank of Sub-lieutenant by virtue of a wizardry at maths that, he had expected, would take him swiftly up the ladder of promotion to become a fully-fledged actuary in short order. But Adolf had other ideas, and here he was, young, smart, his Grammar School background no handicap as it might have once been, using his maths to try to save some Brylcreem Boys from the drink.

'Let me know what you come up with, Pilot. I'll be on the bridge.'

The Pilot nodded, a little absently, already engrossed. He liked being called Pilot and not Sub. Sub-lieutenant Tony Rookes fully intended to rise in the hierarchy of the Royal Navy as he had as an actuary. He fancied he would like to command a destroyer. A real destroyer, not a little dinky toy like *Cormorant*. And as for the skipper saying he'd be on the bridge, it was highly unlikely that whilst they were at sea he'd be anywhere else. Rookes appreciated that.

Dick Mitchell looked at the gyro compass, cocked an eye at the lookouts, saw that Sub-lieutenant Victor Stonegate, the Officer of the Watch, was on his toes, and went to his corner of the bridge. He felt in a discontented frame of mind. This chase was eating up his fuel. If they didn't find the Sunderland within the time Hammerton, the Chief E.R.A., had specified, then they'd have to turn for Belfast and forget the Sunderland.

Then he allowed his thoughts to revert to the subject that had obsessed him since his brief conversation with Angelique Savinien.

Old Baldur!

It had to be him. Had to be. Of course there must be other Baldur Wolz's in Germany – there was a flock of cousins in some romantic old castle or other – but Mitchell knew damn well that the skipper of that particular U-boat was his old friend Baldur Wolz. Old Baldy. Baldur had never demurred at the nickname and

120

Mitchell employed it rarely. Like Ram.

But what a turn up for the book!

He'd stay on his bridge until they found the Sunderland or their fuel reached the return mark. That, at the moment, was all he could do.

'Well?'

Riepold swung about and lowered the Zeiss glasses.

'I'm not sure, skipper.'

That wasn't like Ludwig Riepold at all.

The Second Officer went on, the wind whipping past his face, blowing past Wolz, bringing a scud of driving rain. 'I think it's a Sunderland – or a bit of one.'

Wolz looked. Rain misted the glasses. The sea heaved. Flecks and specks of white laced the heaving surface. Yes. The object could be the half-submerged hull of a big flying boat. The wings must have fallen off. He fancied he could make out the red, white and blue roundel; but the wind slashed rain across his face, and he dragged the glasses away to try to wipe them dry.

'Steer one-oh-five.'

'Steer one-oh-five,' from the helmsman in the tower.

Wolz checked the repeater compass. It would be tricky bringing the boat up in this weather. He just hoped there were no survivors. If there were, he'd probably have to leave them if they could not be brought across rapidly. Where there was one Sunderland there could be another . . .

There would be a little time before they came up with the sinking flying boat. Wolz reflected that Cousin Manfred had been laughingly contemptuous of the Sunderland, claiming his Bf 109 could shoot them down by the baker's dozen.

'Yes, but, Manfred,' Wolz had said, 'we're chugging along at twelve knots or so, not flashing about at five hundred kilometres an hour.'

'Don't believe all you read!'

Manfred was in a most expansive mood. His crushed-down Luftwaffe cap positively sparkled in the early sunshine. Wolz was due to leave the schloss for a few days and he wanted to see as much as he could of Manfred. With the stubborn English making ranting and raving noises, and the future not at all clear, it could well be he wouldn't see Manfred again for some time. They had had some splendid times together as children, the five of them – Helmut, Siegfried, Manfred and himself, and Lisl.

His regular letter from Cousin Lisl told him nothing, as usual. She remained for him unattainable, remote, an image he treasured and dared not even hunger for. She was superb; and he pleasured himself with the Lotties and the Heidis of the world, and entertained serious thoughts about Trudi von Hartstein because she was as near Lisl as anyone might be and yet never attain to the splendour of Cousin Lisl herself . . .

'Cheer up, Baldur! They're bound to give you a boat for yourself now.'

'I hope so.'

He had wondered often enough, and pushed the thought away, what his cousins would say if they knew of his feelings for their sister. Treachery? Contempt? Blazing anger? He did not know and he did not wish to put it to the test.

So they spent a pleasant day together, for Siegfried and the girls had gone early. Manfred simply winked, first thing, and said: 'Your Renate, Baldur. Oh, yes, very nice! My thanks, cousin.'

At least Siegfried had been courteous to Marlene and most attentive to her as they left. Perhaps a sour old sea-dog had managed to mend the rift there. He hoped so. He just did not want to be caught with responsibility for Marlene.

When the time came around for him to catch his train he shook hands with Manfred.

'Mind you shoot down a whole squadron of Spitfires, cousin.'

'Yes. Oh, yes. And you – you torpedo a whole fleet!'

There was a lot in the remark. It brought Wolz up with

a start to a realisation that although wars might differ; their difficulties loomed as large to the men fighting them.

He craned out of the window to see Manfred, trim and immaculate and rakish in his Luftwaffe uniform, the Iron Cross ablaze at his breast pocket. The next time he saw him, he didn't wonder, old Manfred would sport the Ritterkreuz from its ribbon around his neck.

Decorations were being handed out, right enough. He had to admit with a young man's eager acceptance of the standards of his world – with reservations in important areas – that he would muchly like the Eichenlaub zum Ritterkreuz des Eisernen Kreuzes. Yes, very much. But that would have to be earned. Baldur Wolz, sitting back in his seat as the train puffed out, felt that he knew how to earn his decorations in this man's war.

And how grand it would be to see Willi Weidmann again!

Willi was a real scapegrace, a charming inconsequential fellow, and although an affected elegance at times made him appear ludicrous, he was a good sport. They'd served together in U-42 under Kapitänleutnant Gustav Ludecke, and Wolz wanted to know how the skipper was getting on. He'd had a nasty crack on the head and he hadn't been himself since.

He fully intended to break his journey and stop off in Mainz, sample some wines, take a trip on the Rhine, in general stick his neck out seeing all he could all over again.

He'd wired Willi and had suggested they meet later on for an extended trip from Karlsruhe into the Black Forest. That might be most interesting. Certainly, he felt Willi would benefit from decent company again, as he had himself.

The train was crammed with soldiers, all in the relaxed, cheerful mood of men going home on leave. Siegfried had said he'd heard the Army was to be reduced in strength by a fifth, and this had puzzled Wolz. If the Army had won a war, with the Luftwaffe, the Navy were most certainly continuing their own war, a war which had once again become a private affair.

At the Eden Hof he began to book in and, at the sound of his name, the clerk turned and pulled a telegram from the rack. Wolz took it, expecting news that would bring him back to the sea, either with or without a command. The clerk sympathetically took himself off, and Wolz read:

MEET ME BAYERISCHER HOF MUNICH SOONEST URGENT LOTTIE

Wolz frowned. The clerk, watching him, said: 'Not bad news, I trust, Mein Herr?'

'No – just a sudden and unexpected change of plans. I shan't be booking in, after all. Have you a timetable?'

'Here, of course. The war. It changes everything.'

'Yes,' said Wolz, absently, flicking pages.

Lottie had merely to ring his uncle's schloss to find out where he would be staying, and could be certain a telegram would reach him. He wondered what on earth she was doing in Munich. He had no real fears that she might be pregnant; her precautions had always worked admirably.

Anyway, he'd like to see Munich. Have a look around. The night spots should prove interesting, and there was always the beer. He found a good connecting train and went back to the station and booked through. Once more there were soldiers everywhere. As he progressed across Germany south east the usual phenomenon occurred and no one seemed to recognise his uniform, or even to know that Germany possessed a Navy as well as an Army, an Air Force and the SS.

When, at last, the train crawled into Munich, Wolz was feeling very much like a proper sleep in a real bed. At sea, in a U-boat that was always wet, you expected discomfort. The mass of field grey continued to surge about him. At the hotel he went in and looked about the lobby for Lottie. The potted palms, the gilt, the decorations, with the more modern furnishings lent a heavy air to the place and he decided he'd better find a drink

124

quickly. He did not book in, for he had no idea what Lottie was up to. One thing was for sure; he fully intended to enjoy the little romp they would have the moment they were alone.

An aged waiter like a shiny black beetle crept up to him and proffered a silver tray. Wolz took the envelope with a polite thank you. More mystery.

'The lady says she is waiting for you outside, Mein Herr.'

'Thank you.'

The note was a blank sheet of paper in the envelope. Wolz stuck it in his pocket. He was beginning to feel, not so much angry as irritated with his own perplexity. Lottie had always been a great girl, a wonderful romp, and he had no wish to hurt her. But he could not fathom out what she was playing at now.

Outside, the last of the daylight was fading away. A sparse traffic moved on the street, and people were hurrying along. He looked left and right and did not see Lottie. I'll tan her backside for this, he was saying to himself, when a girl approached. She walked easily, with a swing, as though hurrying home before dark. Wolz didn't know her.

As she passed, she whispered: 'Follow me. And don't react.' She kept walking straight on. Wolz forced himself not to spin about and grab her arm and demand an explanation. He stopped himself from blurting out: 'Who are you?'

He carried only a small bag, for he had determined to make this trip simple, and hefting the leather case, he set out after the girl. Even then, through the confusion in his brain, he had to admire the way she walked, a nicely-rounded port and starboard swing, almost but not quite a wobble.

The two men who stepped from a car that drew up outside the Bayerischer Hof wore long black leather overcoats. Their trilby hats were slightly overlarge, and pulled well over their foreheads. Wolz barely gave them a glance, intrigued by the girl.

Of course, this could all be a practical joke of Willi Weidmann's. It was the kind of nonsense that would appeal to that young man.

Around the first corner the light faded dramatically. Shadows lay long over the pavement. A car waited by the kerb, a long low black Mercedes. There was no flag attached to the mast fixed to the front mudguard. The girl slowed. By the car she stopped, turned and bent to speak to the occupant of the front seat, sitting on the passenger side.

Wolz drew level with the car and halted. He prepared to wax exceeding wroth with Lottie – or with Willi.

He looked into the car.

Trudi von Hartstein smiled nervously up at him.

'Tru – ' he started to say, shocked.

She shook her head, quickly, her face white.

'No, no names. Get in, quickly. By me. You must drive.'

'But . . . '

'*Hurry!*'

The girl got in the back. Dazed, Wolz circled the car and settled in the driving seat. He started off, and he drove slowly, and found it extraordinarily difficult to keep his eyes on the road. 'It's late.'

'Yes. There is a house. Drive carefully.'

'You're in trouble?'

'Yes. This is Birgit. She is a friend. Now wait until we are safe.'

Birgit said, suddenly, in a throaty voice: 'There were two just going into the hotel, Karin. We only just missed them.'

About to say: 'Who's Karin,' Wolz stopped, for Trudi von Hartstein said, swiftly: 'They call me Karin. Just drive – Wolfgang.'

Wolfgang! So that's what she called him, this mysterious girl who was shot up in the peaceful German countryside, and now played cops and robbers with the Gestapo. Didn't she understand what she was doing? Wolfgang, indeed!

They reached the house in a quiet suburb and the car rolled gently into the garage and the doors were closed. In the house Trudi took off her hat, which half-shaded her face, and tried to find a smile.

'You're tired, Ba – Wolfgang. We will eat. But first there is someone you must meet.'

Willing now to go along with this melodrama, Wolz was led up the narrow highly-polished wooden stairs. They entered a bedroom. The smell stank.

The man in the bed was not dying, necessarily, if a doctor could attend him. Blood stained the bandages around his chest and on his shoulder. His face looked like that of a sailorman washed up from the sea. Wolz stared.

Birgit laughed and the laugh was a sob.

'I have been trying to doctor Hermann, but – but the bullet was deep.'

At once Wolz took command of himself. He had to master his first intense start of abject fear. Then, swallowing, speaking harshly, he said: 'You took the bullet out?'

'Yes. Poor Hermann.'

The man's breathing moved only shallowly, a series of spasmodic gasps. His chin and cheeks were stubbled yellow.

'He needs a doctor.'

'I am his doctor. I can do all – ' Birgit slumped to her knees by the bed, and took one of the limp hands. 'He must not die.'

'He will recover, Birgit. You will see.' Trudi, who called herself Karin in this household, drew Wolz away. 'Now we will eat and tell Wolfgang what he must do.'

As they descended the stairs, Wolz thought grimly of what Trudi had said. *Must* do . . .

Well, he decided, we shall see.

Over the meal Trudi said: 'I can tell you nothing, save that I desperately need your help. Hermann was to drive. You can see he is incapable.'

'You will tell me nothing?'

The enormity of that infuriated Wolz. But Trudi remained calmly obdurate.

'If you know nothing you can harm no one. I do not think you could find your way to this house again, even though you drove here. I directed you – well, enough of that. Will you drive me?'

'Why can't you drive yourself? You're old enough.'

Birgit let fall an exclamation at this. Trudi motioned her to silence. 'I told you, Birgit, Wolfgang would be my last hope and he would be stubborn. Now you see.'

'Yes, but,' said Wolz. 'Is this criminal? I see it is.'

'No!' flamed Trudi. Her pale face was even more pallid than usual, save when he had carried her on his horse from the blazing car and the burning corpses of her friends. 'No!'

Wolz had decided that he would in all probability ask her to marry him the next time they met. Twice they had met since he had reached that decision, and he had not done so. Somehow she had the knack of bringing up more important matters.

Her golden hair sheened in the light. Her delicate fingers looked thinner than ever. But her figure remained as exciting – more so. She had never looked lovelier in her golden romantic way, charmed and charming, voluptuous in the most moral fashion.

'Will you drive me?'

'Where?'

'Friedrichshafen – the Bodensee.'

Now, Wolz thought, he understood a little more.

'And will you require me to row you across? And you still have not told me why you cannot drive. You have the petrol? The permits?'

'Yes, yes, everything is ready. Everything except the driver. I cannot drive. We will be stopped. It is essential that we use the papers we have.'

'Yes, I see that. And me – Wolfgang – '

She stood up, quickly, and the pallor of her face flushed suddenly and painfully with blood. 'We have Hermann's uniform. It will fit. SS Hauptsturmfuhrer.

It is real. You can carry that off well enough. I have heard the stories about the schloss.'

'Yes, well, when people have themselves a good time others soon get jealous.'

'I thought you – we talked – on the staircase – after –'

She found breathing difficult. Her face alternately flushed and paled. Her breasts moved under the simple grey dress with the little white collar. The buttons were all a tiny shiny black, in twin rows.

'Birgit,' she said. She panted a little, and she would not look at Wolz. 'I think . . . Would you be a dear and leave us alone for a time? There are things that Ba – Wolfgang must know that you need not, just as he must not know – what we know.'

'Yes, Karin. But be careful. Can you trust him?'

Birgit rose and walked to the door. She looked back doubtfully.

'Yes. He is a man of honour. In that I do not misjudge him.'

The door closed with a sharp decisive click behind Birgit.

Wolz looked back at Trudi von Hartstein. Lord, he'd wanted her badly enough. But now he wanted to know what was going on, and knew she would not tell him. He would not guess. That way lay perdition.

She spoke in a soft, low voice that barely carried. Her face was now scarlet from forehead to chin. Her blue eyes regarded him levelly, and then shifted away, and came back to his face again.

'I thought you loved me, Baldur. Perhaps it was merely lust? On the staircase you –'

'I was going to ask you to marry me.'

She gasped. 'Was?'

'It seems you will be in Switzerland whilst I am fighting this war.'

'Ah, Baldur! You hit too hard. It's not like that.'

'No?'

'I see, then, the way you are thinking. Very well, I am

fully prepared to sacrifice a great deal.' As she spoke, her slender fingers began to undo the shiny black buttons. Down one row her fingers crawled like white moths fluttering at a black radiance from some unholy source. The grey material fell away down one side, and she pulled the front of the dress free.

'What – ' began Wolz, shocked.

She stepped out of the dress. She wore white underclothes. She started to strip her chemise off. Her brassiere was white, also, and turned her white flesh by contrast to a subtle pink.

She unclipped the brassiere and threw it across the table.

Wolz caught his breath.

'This is what you want, Baldur. I know. I have seen it. Well, then, take me. Take all the sex you want. We have all night. All night, Baldur, to do as you want with me.' She licked her lips. Her body gleamed in the light, bare and not in the slightest wanton; but full, rich, overpowering. 'Then you will drive me.'

Something in the eerie situation made Wolz in his lightest vein, say: 'If we do as you suggest, I shall be driving you all night.'

The moment he spoke Trudi understood his meaning. She snatched up the dress and held it against her nakedness.

'So you won't – and – '

'Quietly, quietly. I will drive you to the Bodensee. But as for the other – I hungered for you, Trudi, as you can't begin to understand –' How could she? She didn't know about Lisl. 'But you're like an overstrained fiddlestring. If I touched you now you'd snap. Anyway, I need some sleep if we're to motor tomorrow. And you'd better sleep, also.'

She regarded him uncertainly. Her face lost its colour. Her eyes searched his face. Then, with a sob that told Wolz that she understood he meant what he said, she moved forward and put her arms about him. The dress dropped. He could not but feel her against him, feel that

130

warm soft nakedness, as she kissed his cheek.

'Thank you, Baldur. I knew, I knew all along, but –'

'I am going to sleep. You'd better do the same.'

And, as he bunked down on the sofa, Baldur Wolz reflected that he must be the world's biggest idiot to turn down such gorgeously-flaunted beauty. She was better than he'd imagined. There was a future with her, then, after the war, if she got out of this scrape. He resolutely refused to think of Cousin Lisl as his eyes closed and he slept.

'Steer three-four-five.'

'Steer three-four-five.'

That should bring U-55 nicely across the wind and a little heading into it. The sinking Sunderland swashed about in the water, and Baldur Wolz leaned his head down, hunching his shoulders, as a fresh rain squall lashed across. With a slight easement of the rain they were nicely in position. Wind and weather drove them down. He bent to the voicepipe.

'Only a few more tricky bits, Chief. The engine holding out?'

'She'll last your antics, skipper,' came back Loeffler's words. Then: 'Sorry I can't offer you the luxury of two screws.'

'That would have made it easier.'

'Can't see any survivors, skipper,' said Riepold, anxiously. He was anxious for the boat, not the Sunderland's survivors.

'Keep your eyes skinned aloft,' said Wolz in his harsh voice. 'We don't want any of his comrades buzzing us.' The threat was very real. The clouds rolled along bringing the rain with them, and then boiled on towards the east. An aircraft could abruptly appear out of a squall at any time.

His first idea of boarding the flying boat to pick up the cyphers and the secret documents he felt sure she would still be carrying rapidly evaporated. The sea precluded that. Anyway, the Tommies would have ditched all the secret stuff in a lead-weighted bag. He was just wasting time and fuel.

'Steer one-three-oh.' He made up his mind. 'Break off contact with the Sunderland. We're going home.'

CHAPTER FOURTEEN

The gale the crew of U-55 thought to be imminent did not seem to know whether to blow hot or cold. The rain eased, the skies cleared – there was even a brief sight of a patch of blue sky, infinitely far away – and the sea loosened into a longer swell. That rolling movement continued even when the rain slashed back. The weather seemed unable to make up its mind.

'Just like a woman,' observed Ehrenberger with a profound air of the man of the world.

'Quite,' said Wolz.

Women were the most contrary creatures in creation; charming one moment, deadly the next. And naggers ... My God! Hadn't he heard them forever dripping on and on instead of looking straight at the problem. Trudi von Hartstein had looked at her problem straight on. Her driver shot, stranded, she had turned for help to the one man she sensed would respond. She had been unable to contact anyone else, so Wolz understood, and here Birgit's lips had thinned and so he guessed whatever nefarious schemes they had hatched had come adrift.

The journey to the Bodensee was of itself no great problem, given the circumstances of war-time Germany. There would be a strict guard along the frontier, of course; but Trudi said that Wolz need only take her to a certain house and then he could leave.

'And the car?'

'Leave that as well. Once I am with my friends the links will be reforged. It is only now – and you –'

The Mercedes hummed along. Wolz had put an old coat over the SS uniform to drive through Munich and, truthfully enough, he wasn't sure he could find his way back to the house. Now, out on the open road he wore the uniform and, indeed, its mere existence cleared a way for them. The papers were all in order. If they were forged then a master forger had been at work.

Through Landsberg they went and then Trudi insisted they turn off towards Kempten. Away to the south the Alps in their white-capped solitariness shielded countries that were at war and not at war. Italy – well, Wolz, from what he had heard from fellow officers, gathered the Italian U-boat arm were not being trained on the same lines, to put it mildly, as the U-boat arm of the Third Reich. Then, to his fury, Trudi insisted they swing north and go through Wangen.

'But we're nearly at Friedrichshaven, Trudi!'

'Yes. But we're going to Unter-Immenslingen.'

'But that's up towards Uberlingen, right past the Schussen.'

'Yes. We cross the river at Ravensburg – I think the larger town will be easier than Meckenbeuren, say – and the SS Hauptsturmfuhrer must bellow and order if necessary.'

'Like Siegfried – yes, I know.'

So they motored on and were passed and Wolz began to look more keenly at his companion.

They came down through Markdorf and Wolz wondered, now, why he had been such a fool as to turn her down. She really was beautiful. Lottie was beautiful, too, in her own way, as was Heidi. But they were romps. Trudi held a different appeal, something he could not adequately define; but which he felt to be romantic in a sentimental way that was not at all offensive to a rough, tough, womanising U-boat man. That figure! He could see it now, limned against the road, tantalising, alluring –

he really ought to have brought his ship to anchor there!

When, at last, they reached Unter-Immenslingen Trudi directed him to a house, not without a little difficulty. The climate down here was really delightful, almost too hot. The cool air from off the lake helped, and Wolz, incredibly enough, looked aloft in case a Zeppelin should be flying. But, of course, that was from the old days. It was all high-powered monoplanes, with metal monocoque fuselages, these days.

The car was quickly driven from sight into a garage and Wolz, turning to Trudi, found a strange young man with a hard, set face, regarding him balefully. Trudi had vanished.

'You will please come with me.'

Wolz, expecting to meet Trudi later, went.

In the house he was deprived of the SS uniform, given a suit of civilian clothes and papers to go with it claiming he was one Wolfgang Muller, and told to burn clothes and papers the moment he reached Frankfurt.

'Frankfurt?'

'Yes. Now, Herr Wolfgang Muller, is time for you to leave.'

'But – Karin – ?'

'The young lady sends her deepest thanks. She will not forget what you have done.' Tenderness was something very remote from this hard young man. 'Now, please, go. And, I think it hardly necessary to warn you not to speak of this to anyone – not a single person.'

'I won't.'

Feeling not so much angry as betrayed and humiliated, Wolz picked up his bag. If Trudi was in a hurry then she was acting out the part very well. He guessed he would get nothing from this young man, and he did not miss the bulge under his left armpit. And this, in Germany! He was too dazed by the recent events to think clearly. He did remember to look back at the house, and was then struck by its air of neglect. In all probability it was a summer villa of a wealthy Berlin businessman and these people, whoever they were, had borrowed it only so as to receive Trudi. Now they had finished with it, it could moulder on until the end of the war.

No amount of yelling would bring him to her at this moment. And he was abruptly and chillingly aware of what he had been doing. What a fool! Suppose they'd been caught? He'd have been shot, for sure. He sweated as he reached the station; but there was no trouble and in the fullness of time he reached Frankfurt where he would change for Mainz.

Only then did he think of Willi Weidmann.

So that was why he had been told to go to Frankfurt. They knew all about his trip. Trudi had said she had rung the schloss to be told his movements. Her wire had found him. If he'd gone straight to Willi's he might have missed all this.

And if he had? Then what would have happened to Trudi?

So he'd gone on to Willi's and the reaction from his experience had led to moments of great excitement and great enjoyment. Willi told him that Ludecke was apparently back to form and was quite unable to recall his aberrations. U-42 had been on patrol again and – 'Twenty thousand tons, Baldur!'

Wolz had made the usual polite congratulatory noises. He wanted Ludecke to be successful. He did not hold the commander any grudge for diving and leaving Wolz abandoned in his Bachstelze for that had been all the commander could have done in that traumatic moment.

With his leave drawing to an end he bade farewell to the people at the schloss and to Willi, who had gone back with him, and set off for his train.

As he conned U-55 away from the sinking Sunderland he remembered how bitter and how bemused he had been about the whole mad affair with Trudi. He still could not understand it. It had been dangerous. That was horrifically true. What was Trudi up to? Who was she working for? Who were the other people? She had sworn passionately that she was not working against Germany; he had had to settle that at the outset. She had said, with a deep conviction, that she was working for Germany. For the Fatherland. And he believed her.

U-55 tended to be more than a little skittish on the surface with the breeze up her tail. Tomorrow, at the latest, they would have to travel submerged during daylight, just in case.

Now they were at last on the real homeward leg of their patrol Wolz felt it more than ever necessary to ensure the crew kept right up to the mark. Now would be the time for weariness to creep in, a sense that it was already all over, with a consequent lack of attention. That was the way U-boats were lost and their crews killed.

As though in frightening confirmation of that, it was the commander of U-55 himself who made the first sighting.

Wolz, on the bridge in his usual fashion, scanned the whole horizon. The space between the periscope and the bridge coaming was cramped enough; but careful planning and attention to order ensured that the men had room enough. The lookouts appeared to be alert. He had four of them up, with the Officer of the Watch – who happened to be Neitzel – and himself. That was quite enough.

A rain squall drifted away to starboard, an indication the wind was veering. The long straight lines hammered the sea. The smooth rolling swell persisted, with all the fragmented white-caps gone. The day was drawing in. With the cloak of night a U-boatman always felt more comfortable.

A small darker patch showed within the slanting shadowed rain lines. A small, dark patch, growing more definite with each heartbeat. A small, dark patch growing hard and firm into a familiar and dreaded outline.

'Clear the bridge!' bellowed Wolz. 'Jump! Flood! Dive! Dive!'

There was no mistaking that hard sharp prow, that upflung wedge of steel with the flaring white spray-wings to either side.

The lookouts went down the ladder like ferrets. Neitzel, without even a single glance at his skipper, followed, treading on the hands of the man beneath him, roaring at him to get on.

Last off his bridge, Wolz heard the single diesel bellow throatily through the exhaust as the obermaschinist in the engine room shoved it up to full power. The man had to get them moving if they were to dive speedily; and then the cut-off had to be brought in at exactly the right moment for the air intake to be chopped and the electric motors to be switched in.

The English destroyer was close on them – too close for comfort. The treacherous rain squalls provided perfect cover. There was the logical chance that the Englishman would be as surprised as the German.

U-55 was going down.

The Chief had her now, driving her on with planes set hard for diving, the sea smashing into the ballast tanks. A roaring tumultuous few moments as the spray sliced across the bridge and the boat slid away below him, and then Wolz had his feet into the opened hatch and was falling down the ladder.

He reached up and grabbed the wheel set in the centre of the heavy steel hatch, turned it fast.

Familiar noises surrounded him as he dropped to the conning tower deck. The helmsman stood phlegmatically. The boat trembled. She was going down.

The Chief kept one eye on the depth gauges, one eye on the inclinometer – and if he had another eye that was checking the telltales as each tank flooded from forward to aft.

Wolz dropped through into the control room. A single fleeting glance around told him that everyone was at their station. Loeffler murmured a word or two to the planesman. The depth gauge needles spun around. They were going down sharply, as the inclinometer testified.

'Level at one hundred metres,' said Wolz.

Over the familiar thrum of the U-boat's machinery a

137

new and dreadfully familiar sound obtruded.

Like a railway train scything through the sky above their heads, the whirring, pulsing, roaring sound of the destroyer approached, growing and growing in intensity.

Any minute now . . .

Instinctively, without realising they were doing it, some of the men looked up. Most bent their heads a little, as though about to step out into a torrential downpour.

The smell of the boat came to Wolz then, in that frozen moment, heady with its aromas and stinks.

The depthcharges kerrumped twice.

U-55 shivered a little. The lights flickered. Then they were easing off at a hundred metres, and the first attack was over almost before they'd set themselves for its onset.

'Miles away,' said Wolz. He made his voice boom with confidence.

Ping!

Ping, ping, ping!

The rustle scraped across their steel hull, and went away, and returned.

Ping!

'Port ninety!'

'Port ninety!'

U-55 swung northwards.

'Full revolutions.'

'Group up, full revolutions.'

Wolz waited, not counting the passing heartbeats but letting the feel of his boat, the sense of her in the water, the dwindling rushing roar of the destructive engine over his head, all merge and mingle and tell him when to order the next evasive action.

'Stop starboard. Make two knots. Silent routine. Steer oh-nine-oh.'

A hush fell on U-55.

The men would have to sweat over the controls now, for the electric power would be cut under the routine of silent running. Not a sound – Wolz had dinned it into their heads enough times – not a sound. Your lives depend on it . . .

The ping rustled away.

Loeffler let out a long silent breath. A drop of perspiration fell from his broad nose.

How smart was the captain up aloft? wondered Wolz. Had U-55 avoided him so easily?

Or was this merely the beginning of a long-drawn out battle of wits?

Ping! from the asdic hut.

Just that. Ping. Not an echo or anything like an echo.

'Keep trying,' said Lieutenant Commander Dick Mitchell. 'He's down there somewhere.'

No one on the bridge of H.M.S. *Cormorant* cared to point out to the skipper that there was an awful lot of sea water down there as well. Needles and haystacks were easy meat by comparison.

The brief glimpse Mitchell had had of the U-boat before she dived had shown she was travelling south east. Going home, back to the brand new bases the Nazis had fixed up for themselves along the French Atlantic coast. So it was a good guess the bastard would turn that way after he'd been missed by that first fumbled attack. Two charges had gone down. *Cormorant* could tumble the depthcharges off her stern with fair rapidity; but her throwers needed too much time, in Mitchell's opinion, to be reloaded.

'Starboard thirty. Steer one-three-oh.'

Cormorant heeled. She swung through the sea, her slim shape cutting through the swell and spouting water up greenly, swashing a broad smooth wake as she turned.

'Midships. Steady on one-three-oh.'

The monotonous ping from asdic did not change.

Come on, come on, you bastard! Mitchell stood, steadily, four square, by the compass platform. His mind was attuned to the movements of his ship, the scend of the sea, the wind, the whole living vibrating fabric of his command. Down there, somewhere, a U-boat skipper was feeling very much the same sensations. Mitchell dearly wanted to drop a couple of charges alongside the fellow's ears. He'd already seen burning and sinking merchantmen, and felt the helplessness. And he'd spoken to survivors. He had a party of survivors aboard now . . .

He refused to let his thoughts even remotely contemplate Angelique Savinien. She was beautiful, a girl from out of another part of his life, brutally catapulted into this half; no, his whole life was bound up with that U-boat down there.

'He's got to be somewhere!' he said, again, and choked back what else he might have said.

The search for the Sunderland would now be definitely abandoned. His fuel was already nudging the danger mark. Hammerton was most unhappy. This high-speed manoevring would eat up their supplies. If he couldn't nail the U-boat quickly, they would never catch her.

His grim thoughts had reached that conclusion when the signal came in. He kept his lean face expressionless.

The Sunderland's crew had been taken off by a destroyer which, by pure chance, had passed within hailing distance. Had that signal been routed half an hour earlier, then *Cormorant* would never have stumbled across the U-boat.

'Have to be thankful for small mercies, sir,' said Number One.

'Yes.'

The asdic hut continued to report no contact.

'Steer oh-eight-oh.'

The fellow down there might be chuckling away to himself, on a course to safety, thinking he wouldn't turn directly for the French coast but head a little south or north of the bearing. That way he'd lose his pursuer for sure.

Cormorant turned on to the new course. Mitchell remained silent. Number One looked at his skipper, and went back to being Number One with a conscious attention. This kind of operation was all in favour of the

140

U-boat. The asdic could help enormously and the man on the set, Atkins, was very good. But it was all a matter of flair. Dick Mitchell had not proved himself in combat yet; Number One just hoped the skipper would prove to contain that flair along with his maniacal way of living.

Another signal was taken in. The destroyer was turning to join *Cormorant*. Mitchell drew his brows down. This was his U-boat! If this hustling great destroyer came barging in and took the prize from under his nose!

A ghostly rustle sounded on the heels of the next ping.

The asdic hut did not report.

Atkins was waiting for the next one.

Mitchell opened his mouth.

The ping and its echo of a tinnier ping crackled like lightning.

'Contact, sir. Red nine-oh. Going right.'

Instantly Mitchell brought *Cormorant* around in a sharp heel to port. He'd been right! The tricky bastard had taken off due east. The pings and the answering echoes continued to pour from the asdic hut and Mitchell felt the mood of the bridge change. Now they were expectant, where before they had been resigned to defeat.

'Four charges.'

He waited.

The asdic couldn't give him the depth and he would have to make a lightning-quick mental calculation when the asdic lost contact. In that moment of silence as the sloop ran on over the target he was deaf to what was going on below. But the distance ahead at which they lost contact would give him an estimation of the depth.

Ping-ping! Ping-ping!

The depth-charge party aft reported all ready, standing by. They had closed up to action stations with commendable rapidity at the first alarm. They would do their job. It was up to the skipper to make sure their eggs went down into the right place.

The Commissioned Torpedo Gunner, Mr Herbert,

had licked his depth-charge party into good shape. Like all escorts, they prided themselves on the shortness of time they took to reload.

'Lost contact, ahead, sir!'

Mitchell compressed his lips, held motionless for two heartbeats, and then said, crisply: 'Set charges for one fifty.'

Now Mr Herbert would be tested, getting the fuses set on the charges before they were hurled from the throwers or trundled over the stern . . .

Mitchell would have liked to drop more than four; but he had a limited supply and no really rapid method of distributing them. If he missed the bastard this time then he'd drop six next time . . . Then, one more try and that would be it.

Cormorant ran forward over the cone of silence. At precisely the right moment the depthcharges flew into the air or rolled over her stern. Four canisters of death sank swiftly through the depths.

The shattering force of the explosions hammered U-55 down as though trodden underfoot by a giant. Cautiously coming up, Wolz caught the pinging against his hull and turned at once. Only his depth saved him.

Driven down, flung from side to side, rocked and wrenched and shaken, U-55 reeled in the depths.

The lights burst in showers of glass fragments. The dials crazed over as though stricken by frost. The emergency lighting came on, tiny bulbs pallidly illuminating the vital areas of the boat and leaving gloomy shadows elsewhere that might be peopled by ghosts.

Men yelled. The hull shook. Water spurted. U-55 lurched crazily.

Gripping on to a dark projection that cut cruelly into his fingers, Wolz fought to stay on his feet. His command was being savaged. And he met that savagery by a savage determination to stay alive.

'Full ahead both!'

U-55 responded; but sluggishly, coming out of the

142

abandonment of the corkscrewing motion.

The depthcharges had been accurately-placed. Their depth-setting had been too high. A few more metres on the fuses, and U-55 would be sinking to the Atlantic seabed, shattered, with air bubbling from her ruptured seams.

'That fellow up there is a devil.' Wolz checked himself. He must not allow an overpowering personality to the English captain. He was just a man trying to kill him. As the boat sorted itself out and fresh bulbs were screwed in and the water was shut off, Wolz reflected that if the man who was trying to kill him could not be regarded as some kind of personality, he must, indeed, be a very devil.

U-55 crept away.

The pings held her.

The beat of the destroyer's propellers fluctuated, dwindled, and then resumed their hateful roaring rushing approach.

'Take her down, Chief!' bellowed Wolz.

The boat drove for the deeper depths.

This time there were six explosions, although they blended into a concussing roar. The boat shook . . . The lights ruptured again, and the petty officers went about screwing in fresh. Water sloshed underfoot.

'Number three pump!' said Loeffler. 'It's that valve-fitting – she'll break on us the moment we blow – I can feel it.'

Wolz was perfectly prepared to believe the Chief.

'Level.' He spoke harshly. 'We'll blow with what we have when we have to.'

Men were screaming from forward.

'Find out what that is, Neitzel.'

There was no ready response of: 'Very good, skipper!' 'Neitzel!'

In the patchy illumination Wolz looked around. The splintered faces of dials leered at him. Water dripped from fractured pipes where the valves had been cut off. Men's faces showed gaunt, darkly-bearded, corpse-like.

143

'Neitzel!'

The men continued screaming from forward.

The heavy watertight doors were shut.

Wolz slapped the voicepipe cover.

'Forward? What's the trouble?'

The voice of the leading torpedoman.

'It's Leicht, Herr Oberleutnant.'

The man sounded as though he was only just keeping down panic.

'Yes?'

'A rivet – sprung – ripped into his guts, skipper – blood all over the place!'

'See to it! Make him comfortable.'

Wolz swung back.

'Herr Leutnant Neitzel!'

Ehrenberger bent to the watery deck. He slipped and recovered. He came up grasping a limp and sodden bundle.

'He's cracked, skipper! I don't think he's dangerous, but . . .'

'Restrain him if you have to! Steer one-eight-oh. Group up, full revolutions. Get some light over here. Chief – '

Loeffler was staring at the depth gauges, knocking away splintered friezes of glass.

'Yes, skipper. We're still going down – two hundred –'

'Level, I said.'

The Chief stiffened. He bellowed swift and precise instructions, and compressed air hissed. The inclinometer indicated they were bows down.

'Forward torpedoroom,' snapped Wolz. 'Have you shipped water? How much?'

The sounds of Hans Leicht in the background formed a distressing accompaniment to the answer.

Wolz almost lost the reply, as a long ululating howl burst from the crazed figure of Neitzel. He reared up, flinging Ehrenberger off. He made a mad lunge for the ladder leading to the conning tower.

Ehrenberger recovered and jumped after him.

Riepold, suddenly appearing, hit Neizel flush along the jaw.

The Third Officer collapsed. His head hit the metal ladder with a soggy meaty thunk.

'If you've killed him, Ludwig,' said Wolz, 'he died in action. Chief! You'll have to blow. We're flooding forrard. Blow!'

'Very good!'

'Stand by gun crew.'

Number three pump wheezed and groaned like a punctured church organ. Wolz bent down beside the Chief, who edged sideways and they both peered over the shoulder of the rating at the depth gauges. They hung. The red needle quivered around two hundred. U-55 struggled.

'She's got to go up – she's got to!'

Stupid to think that if he hadn't hit Forstner and his bully boys with the valve-fitting they wouldn't be in this deadly predicament. The Chief would have checked the fitment before using it. But the macabre thought persisted in Wolz's brain. And, all the time, the ping-ping-ping echoed like skeletal claws from their hull, a ghastly summoning knocking every ten seconds.

U-55 hung in the deeps, precariously perched between life and death.

CHAPTER FIFTEEN

H.M.S. *Cormorant* came around in a roaring bucking circle. Spray whipped back drenching the men forward, reaching to the tiny bridge and soaking Mitchell and everyone there. A rain squall blotted down, turning the last of the daylight into an inky presage of night.

'Godammit! The fellow's there! We must have hit him!'

The sea was beginning to crest, and even in the beginning darkness the razored-tops of the waves showed whitecaps. *Cormorant* could not keep up her twenty knot speed in too much of a seaway. The elements were taking a hand in favour of the U-boat now.

An Aldiss lamp blinked aggressively at them. Mitchell could just make out the lean dark shape of H.M.S. *Valkyrie* as she passed across *Cormorant's* bows. He felt very much like shaking a fist at the destroyer.

'Acknowledge.' Mitchell spoke sharply. 'Make to *Valkyrie*: "Have four charges left. Then she's all yours." Oh, yes, and add: "Good hunting." '

'Aye aye, sir.'

The wraithlike shape of *Valkyrie* blinked back an acknowledgment. She might only be an old V and W, built by Denny in '17 and due to be pensioned off; but she made *Cormorant* look the tiny and fragile craft the little sloop was. *Valkyrie* had had her forward boiler and uptake taken out and extra bunkers fitted. Her four 4-inch L.A. guns had been replaced by four 4-inch H.A. guns. Her six torpedo tubes had gone. She was a long-range escort destroyer now and the Navy could do with a hundred more like her.

The filthy night clamped down. The sea rose. The pings continued from the asdic hut; but, as he had known would happen in this kind of sea, very soon asdic reported contact lost. Asdic just did not work very well in rough conditions. Somewhere beneath him the U-boat was lurking about, trying to escape, and now he was absolutely deaf – no! No, by God! Not quite . . .

'Blowing sounds, sir. Loud.'

Switched to a hydrophone role, the instruments were picking up unmistakable sounds of a U-boat blowing tanks.

'He's coming up! Number One! Close up gun crew.

146

If he surfaces anywhere near us I want to put a few bricks into him before he even has time to open his hatch!'

'Aye aye, sir.'

It would be no picnic on the wildly-tossing sloop to bring the forward four-incher into action. But the men would do it. They were fired with the same kind of animosity as their captain.

'Where's *Valkyrie*! Guns – make damn sure you don't shoot at her.' Then, the old maniacal Dick Mitchell breaking out, he added: 'She might shoot back and she has more guns than we have.'

'Aye aye, sir.'

Then a lookout: 'U-boat! Red ninety!'

Everybody swung to look. The barrels of the forward four-incher and the non-regulation two-pounder aft began to traverse to port.

'Belay gun action!' bellowed Mitchell after a single look. 'That's *Valkyrie*! Lookout, you're on First Lieutenant's report.'

A lashing torrent of rain swept across the bridge. Water ran from Mitchell's face and soaked into his collar. He shook his head angrily and peered again at *Valkyrie*. The destroyer started to blink a signal, and he cursed. 'What's he keep chattering for?'

And so, blaspheming against that distant spark from the Aldiss, Mitchell saw the slender shape dark in passing silhouette. The reprimanded lookout up on the First Luff's orders saw it, too. He yelled, and this time an injured note of innocence rang in his voice.

'U-boat! Red seventy – and the bloody thing's there!'

'Hard a-port!' screamed Mitchell. 'We'll ram the bastard!'

In a raging sea, heeling wildly, spray pelting over her, the little sloop swung towards the surfaced U-boat.

Number three pump ground to uselessness just as U-55 began to lift. The tenseness drew harsh lines on all the crew's faces. Perspiration soaked them. Agonisingly,

U-55 lifted. And then, as though a miracle occurred, the probing maddening fingers knocking and rustling against the hull ceased.

'His detection apparatus has lost us,' said Ehrenberger. He spoke as though making a formal report on parade. But Baldur Wolz understood only too well.

'Take us up, Chief.'

Wolz led the rush up the conning tower. He bashed the hatch open and sprang on to the bridge. Rain razored over his face, blinding him, making him gasp. The darkness stretched all about him – and, in the darkness, the bows of a destroyer swinging towards him, her long low rakish hull just vanishing beyond the upflung comb of spray.

'Full ahead on both – starboard!' he screamed and the single diesel picked up with a rumbling roar. 'Hard a-port!'

U-55 began to surge through the water and to turn to port. The waves battered her, lifting her and dropping her with sickening lurches that shivered through her narrow hull.

The gun crew clustered at the foot of the ladder awaiting orders to race on to the deck and man the 8.8 centimetre. Wolz looked at the sleeting rain scything the deck, the way his boat shivered and corkscrewed. A man would be washed overboard down on the casing. Steinback harnesses . . . He watched the enemy destroyer and prayed she'd miss. One glancing blow and they'd both be done for in this weather . . .

Riepold let out a yell.

'Another destroyer! Ahead of us, broadside on – '

Wolz swung to look. He clamped up his mouth.

'Empty tubes, empty tubes – '

Now U-55 was turning fast and faster. Having got way on the boat he ordered half speed reverse on the port motor. With the starboard engine thrusting them on and the port motor turning them, they spun around in the ugly sea.

U-55 lay over with a list in the sea that was not caused

by their turn. Some of the tanks had not fully blown, then. That number three . . .

The Chief was doing what he could; but the boat bucked and rolled and pitched as she veered. Spray burst clean across the conning tower. The destroyer scythed past. Neither vessel fired, for U-55's gun was not manned and the destroyer could not depress her forward gun sufficiently.

The darkness clamped.

'What's the second destroyer doing?'

The bridge lookouts shielded their eyes from the weather and tried to peer into the fitful darkness.

Two enemies made life infinitely more difficult.

Water surged and crashed darkly along the casing and washed viciously around the gun. Water slashed at the men on the bridge. Wolz bent to shield his face, yelling: 'When can we dive, Chief? There are two of the beauties up here now.'

'Give me five minutes, skipper – '

'Make it four and a half, Chief!'

U-55 circled.

Still the rain lashed in patchy drenchings that thinned away and left a fragmentary visibility. The night was building up into a gale. Madness, for men to be trying to kill each other in slender steel ships when they should be battening all down snug to ride out the gathering storm.

Groping through the half-darkness, battered, drenched, staggering, the three vessels weaved their patterns across the hostile sea.

If only he could dive!

Once below the surface in this weather the U-boat would be safe from the destroyers. Wolz knew that. The Chief knew it, too, and Loeffler drove his team and himself to put U-55 into diving trim once more.

Through one of those tantalising breaks in the curtains of rain Wolz spotted the sleek dark shape with the foam of white breaking all along the hull, from bow to stern.

He did not know which one of the destroyers that was – he didn't care. One had seemed larger than the other; but they both killed U-boats, if they were given the chance.

Solid water broke black and green all along the forward casing and smashed waist deep around the gun. The water slammed into the conning tower, shaking the U-boat, sending shudders through her steel frame. Water boiled and cascaded aft, sluicing over the saddle tanks where the sea roiled in hungrily.

They were not riding anywhere near as high as they might; trimmed well down through the tons of water that had driven in through the distorted plating. The Chief and his men had to sort the forward compartment out before they could dive. And meanwhile U-55 lurched and rolled and twisted like a half-submerged log, and two English destroyers ran and hunted eagerly through the rain-shrouded darkness.

In that claustrophobic moment when the Englishman had almost rammed, Wolz had taken the fleeting chance to size up his antagonist. She looked like a destroyer; but he had seen the size of her. U-55 as a type VIIB was sixty-six and a half metres long; the English-man was only a few metres longer, far shorter than a regular destroyer. She carried just a single gun on her fo'c'sle. Wolz recognised her. She was a Kingfisher class patrol sloop. So that meant she was a knot or two faster than U-55. He gave his orders with care.

'Aft torpedo room. Shallow setting.' The King-fishers had only two metres draught. In this sea the chance that an eel would porpoise or dive deep or do anything stupid was very high; but Wolz was determined. At the first chance he would loose. At the very least it would give the Englishman a fright, might make him draw off long enough to give the Chief time enough.

Water broke spuming over the bridge and ran down through the hatch. If this went on they'd have to shut up. U-55 could be sunk just as swiftly by the sea as by depthcharges.

'Aft tube flooded!'

He was all set. Now U-55 would go hunting.

The displacement of the Kingfishers was just over five hundred tons as compared with U-55's standard displacement surfaced of 753 and submerged of 857. Wolz considered the figures without cheer. Twelve hundred gross registered tons was the target. Neither of these destroyers, he thought, would give him that.

'Destroyer!' yelped a lookout. Then: 'Starboard beam. Range five hundred.'

A parting veil of rain, a fractional lightening, and the hard sharp silhouette of the destroyer broke through. She was a V and W class. Wolz's broad mouth firmed. This was it.

'Hard a port! Aft torpedo room. Stand by.'

He'd shoot this one by eye. With the violent motion of the boat, corkscrewing, rolling, pitching, leaping about like a crazed salmon, he would have to judge his moment to perfection.

U-55 lurched around in the sea.

Enormous competence as seamen was required now of all three captains. The wild motions of their commands rendered everything they did ten times more difficult. The patchy darkness was treacherous. The continuous motion dragged at nervous energy, drained a man of strength and the capacity for rapid decision. Tenacity, determination, absolute professionalism, dedication – these were the qualities demanded now.

Wolz watched with a fine-tuned sensitiveness. He was a U-boatman to his fingertips. And this was where he proved it.

'*Loose!*'

U-55 shuddered to a fresh and familiar thump among the wild battering of the sea. The aft torpedo leaped from the tube, scythed through the waves, running shallow, running dead for the engine room of the English destroyer.

Lieutenant Commander Jimmy Watt, known to his

irreverent contemporaries as Old Boiler, thumped the bridge coaming, glaring across the rain-swept, wind-lashed sea.

'What's the fool playing at?'

For *Cormorant* appearing like a spuming ghost from the swirling veils of rain, bore down on *Valkyrie* like a runaway train.

The destroyer rolled and bucked and twisted. The waves smashed at her thin plating. *Cormorant* vanished for a moment and then re-appeared belting along, smothered in foam, plunging deep, lifting with a greyly-white frieze of spume spouting aft.

'High-speed propeller effect!'

The asdic hut's report swung every eye to port.

In the confusing wish-wash of streaks, in the smothering and lifting darkness, the track of the torpedo could just be made out.

'Hard a-port! Full ahead starboard. Half astern port.'

Valkyrie began to turn. But Watt knew he would never get his command out of the way of that deadly kipper in time.

Now he saw what *Cormorant* was up to. He knew her commander, that maniac Ram Mitchell.

'Come on, Ram!' breathed Watt. 'You can do it...'

Dick Mitchell blinked rainwater and flying scud away from his eyes. The dark tumbled water seethed as *Cormorant* lay right over, heeling incredibly on a tight inswinging turn.

Out of the flying muck the U-boat had appeared and he'd turned instantly and then, as the flying spume and rain parted momentarily, *Valkyrie* was revealed, broadside on to the U-boat's stern.

Through all the welter of spume and rain and flying scud Mitchell saw the thin betraying track of the torpedo just beneath the surface.

They were on a collision course.

Jolting as though they rode over a corrugated surface, battered, drenched, hanging on grimly, the men on the bridge of the little sloop saw the U-boat, saw the torpedo, saw *Valkyrie* – and saw, too, their own bows swinging into the path of destruction.

'You've got to hand it to him,' yelled Number One. Lieutenant Andy Stevens turned his water-shining face towards his skipper.

'Yes. And I'll hand it to him right up his backside!' snarled Mitchell.

But Number One was right. The U-boat had done it all right, incredibly right. She'd outwitted *Valkyrie*, for sure, and as *Cormorant* flew and swooped over the waves Mitchell was debating the best methods of picking up survivors. He could get them inboard all right after the destroyer sank – if the U-boat let him.

He fancied the kipper should pass beneath *Cormorant's* keel. The sloop drew so little water the chances of a strike in this weather were remote. He held on. His ship hurled towards the U-boat. On the crazily bucking forecastle the gun-crew went through the drill in near-impossible conditions. The four-incher banged off. The smoke was instantly picked up and shredded and smashed away into nothingness. Where the shell went, God alone knew.

The torpedo struck H.M.S. *Cormorant* just abaft the bows.

The wave lifted the deadly missile at the last moment so that instead of passing safely beneath the keel where the contact pistol would be useless, the kipper lifted and smashed into the fragile steel plating. The massive explosion lifted the little sloop, threw men to the deck, knocked the gun-crew staggering, slashed a ripped-open hole and gouted a toppling plume of white water over and on to the bridge.

Spluttering, gasping, raging, Mitchell dragged himself to his feet.

'Stop both!' he bellowed.

Already his ship had scooped tons of sea water. She was down by the head. She was going – and going fast. Her whole bows were blown away in the blast.

Only one order could be given now. And it had to be given fast.

'*Abandon ship!*'

All the things he must do flooded up into his mind. The ship tilted. She was going. Men were roaring up on to the deck. Floats went over as lines were cut. In the confusing darkness many men might die if they were not picked up quickly – *would* die.

As he waited for everyone to clear his sinking command, Dick Mitchell stared across at *Valkyrie*. She would see what had happened and come nosing in to pick them up. There was a very good chance for his crew and his survivors even in this sea.

The Jerry U-boat had fired the kipper from her stern tubes.

The U-boat was going away. She would not be able to shoot again from her single stern tube, and she was making no attempt to turn to bring her four bow tubes into action. They were probably empty, for the boat was on a course to take her back to base.

At last everyone was clear. Mitchell checked the bridge. He was alone. He went to the side and climbed up ready to jump. Poor old *Cormorant* was surging sluggishly now, bows down, what was left of them. She'd be gone in only moments more.

As he jumped he thought that the skipper of the U-boat was a very smart cookie. Very smart indeed.

Just before he hit the water to be picked up, the blazing thought hit him.

Suppose that had been Baldur Wolz?

Suppose it had been? Just think!

Well, Mitchell told himself as he was hoisted in over the edge of the Carley raft, well, old son, next time it will be my turn.

The moment he loosed the eel Baldur Wolz knew it would hit. Everything had gone right. Then, from nowhere, parting the dark veils of rain like some rearing phantom, the other little destroyer pounced. She bore in smothered in spray and instantly Wolz realised what she was trying to do. But that eel was running . . . It was going to hit something . . .

He whipped his glasses up. The dots of men's heads showed on the bridge. One of those little dots was the captain and he was taking his little ship in to take on the torpedo and then U-55. A gun cracked from forward and the shell added a brief flicker of white to the sea alongside.

'Full ahead on engine and both motors! Chief, give me all you've got!'

U-55 surged ahead. She lifted and dropped on the angry sea. The destroyer, and Wolz knew she was really only a little patrol sloop, suddenly lifted in the water. She reared her bows up. The explosion cracked viciously across the water. The bows of the little ship blew apart. Almost at once she started to go down by the head.

Some idiot below in the pressure hull of U-55 started to cheer.

'We got him!' someone else yelled, his voice a thin shriek over the wind and the waves and the slashing downpour of the rain. Wolz half-turned, not taking his eyes off the sinking English ship. It was von Magdorf, shouting, his wet face shining.

Well, he might turn out all right, now that he'd seen some action and the influence of Neitzel was removed.

The Chief reported.

'You can take her down now, skipper, whenever you like.'

Wolz looked back. The destroyer, who had been saved from certain destruction by the actions of the sloop, was curving in, ready to pick up survivors. Wolz just hoped that the captain of the English sloop was among them. He was a courageous man. Mentally, Wolz doffed his white commander's cap to his enemy opposite number. He did not suppose he would ever find out who it was. But that did not matter. Two adversaries had met and fought, and Baldur Wolz had won.

155

'Take her down, Chief. Flood! Dive! Dive!'

Last down his conning tower, slamming the heavy steel hatch shut and spinning the wheel, Wolz took his steel shark back to the dark depths which were her natural home.

Safely below the surface, on course back to base, Wolz found his chief regret echoed by Ehrenberger. The First Officer rubbed his bearded chin, saying: 'Almost fifty thousand, skipper. That last little runt won't make it up – a pity.'

'Yes, Kern, a pity. But it's still a great total. A great victory.'

Wolz looked at the familiar interior of his U-boat, the pipes and dials – their glasses shivered to fragments – the levers and shining equipment. The familiar close stink wafted to his nostrils. He looked at his men. Yes, they had performed well, when it came down to it.

But this war was nowhere near over yet, despite what the propaganda machine fed the people back home. Wolz had not missed the ferocity of those destroyers' attacks. England was not yet beaten. That was for the future. And Baldur Wolz, Oberleutnant zur See of the U-boat arm of the Kriegsmarine of the Third Reich, knew that he would be in the thick of the fight.

As U-55 slid through the deeps on her way back to base he knew that he would not wish to be anywhere else.

For Baldur Wolz, the long war was just beginning.

THE GUNN SERIES BY JORY SHERMAN

GUNN #1: DAWN OF REVENGE   (590, $1.9.

Accused of killing his wife, William Gunnison changes his name to Gunn and begins his fight for revenge. He'll kill, maim, turn the west blood red—until he finds the men who murdered his wife.

GUNN #2: MEXICAN SHOWDOWN   (628, $1.95)

When Gunn rode into the town of Cuchillo, he didn't know the rules. But when he walked into Paula's cantina he knew he'd learn them. And he had to learn fast—to catch a ruthless killer who'd murdered a family in cold blood!

GUNN #3: DEATH'S HEAD TRAIL   (648, $1.95)

When Gunn stops off in Bannack City, he finds plenty of gold, girls and a gunslingin' outlaw. With his hands on his holster and his eyes on the sumptuous Angela Larkin, Gunn goes off hot—on his enemy's trail!

GUNN #4: BLOOD JUSTICE   (670, $1.95)

Gunn is enticed into playing a round with a ruthless gambling scoundrel. He also plays a round with the scoundrel's estranged wife—and the stakes are on the rise!

GUNN #5: WINTER HELL   (708, $1.95)

Gunn's journey west arouses more than his suspicion and fear. Especially when he comes across the remains of an Indian massacre—and winds up with a ripe young beauty on his hands . . .

GUNN #6: DUEL IN PERGATORY   (739, $1.95)

Someone in Oxley's gang is out to get Gunn. That's the only explanation for the sniper on his trail. But Oxley's wife is out to get him too—in a very different way.

GUNN #7: LAW OF THE ROPE   (766, $1.95)

The sheriff's posse wants to string Gunn up on the spot—for a murder he didn't commit. And the only person who can save him is the one who pointed the finger at him from the start: the victim's young and luscious daughter!

Available wherever paperbacks are sold, or order direct from the Publisher. Send cover price plus 50¢ per copy for mailing and handling to Zebra Books, 475 Park Avenue South, New York, N.Y. 10016. DO NOT SEND CASH.

WORLD WAR II—
FROM THE GERMAN POINT OF VIEW

SEA WOLF #1: STEEL SHARK   (755, $2.25)
by Bruno Krauss
The first in a gripping new WWII series about the U-boat war
waged in the bitter depths of the world's oceans! Hitler's crack
submarine, the U-42, stalks a British destroyer in a mission that
earns ruthless, ambitious Baldur Wolz the title of "Sea Wolf"!

SEA WOLF #2: SHARK NORTH   (782, $2.25)
by Bruno Krauss
The Fuhrer himself orders Baldur Wolz to land a civilian on the
deserted coast of Norway. It is winter, 1940, when the U-boat
prowls along a fjord in a mission that could be destroyed with
each passing moment!

SEA WOLF #3: SHARK PACK   (817, $2.25)
by Bruno Krauss
Britain is the next target for the Third Reich, and Baldur Wolz is
determined to claim that victory! The killing season opens and the
Sea Wolf vows to gain more sinkings than any other sub in the
Nazi navy . . .

*Available wherever paperbacks are sold, or order direct from the
Publisher. Send cover price plus 50¢ per copy for mailing and
handling to Zebra Books, 475 Park Avenue South, New York,
N.Y. 10016. DO NOT SEND CASH.*

TROUBLE SHOOTING WESTERNS

BOLT #1: FIRST BLOOD (767-8, $2.25)
by Cort Martin

Jared Bolt is tricked into a wild wench's bed—but he's damned if he's going to be tricked into wedding her! The reverend's son would rather be an outlaw, gambling for money, and never too far from trouble—or women!

BOLT #2: DEAD MAN'S BOUNTY (783-X, $2.25)
by Cort Martin

A price on his head and three bounty hunters on his tail make Jared Bolt light out of town. It's not too long before pistols are smoking and two men lay dying. When Bolt heads to his lady Cassie for a little tender loving care, he finds only a ransom note—and the ransom is Bolt himself!

THE SCOUT #1: ROWAN'S RAIDERS (754-6, $2.50)
by Buck Gentry

Six years in the camps of the fierce, savage Oglala Sioux, trained Eli Holten to be an expert in hunting, tracking—and killing. Now, as an Army wagon commander in the wilderness, the Scout rides each danger-filled mile as if it were his last . . .

THE SCOUT #2: DAKOTA MASSACRE (794-5, $2.50)
by Buck Gentry

After a brutal Sioux surprise attack, Eli Holten's instincts tell him the massacre was too much a surprise. Army deserters masquerading as deadly Indians are the culprits, and the Scout won't take things lying down—especially when his lady is held hostage and his name is at stake . . .

Available wherever paperbacks are sold, or order direct from the Publisher. Send cover price plus 50¢ per copy for mailing and handling to Zebra Books, 475 Park Avenue South, New York, N.Y. 10016. DO NOT SEND CASH.